JF HOLUB
Holub, Joan, author.
Idun and the apples of youth

W9-BFC-052

Idun and the Apples of Youth

ALSO BY
JOAN HOLUB & SUZANNE WILLIAMS

Don't miss the latest books in the
Goddess Girls series!
Medea the Enchantress
Eos the Lighthearted
Clotho the Fate

Check out the most recent books in the
Heroes in Training series!
Dionysus and the Land of Beasts
Zeus and the Dreadful Dragon
Hercules and the Nine-Headed Hydra

Read more books in the Thunder Girls series!
Freya and the Magic Jewel
Sif and the Dwarfs' Treasures

Coming soon:
Skade and the Enchanted Snow

Be sure to read the Little Goddess Girls series!
Athena & the Magic Land
Persephone & the Giant Flowers

Coming soon:
Aphrodite & the Gold Apple

Thunder Girls

BOOK 3

Idun and the
Apples of Youth

JOAN HOLUB &
SUZANNE WILLIAMS

Fountaindale Public Library
Bolingbrook, IL
(630) 759-2102

Aladdin

New York   London   Toronto   Sydney   New Delhi

This book is a work of fiction. Any references to historical events, real people, or real places are used fictitiously. Other names, characters, places, and events are products of the author's imagination, and any resemblance to actual events or places or persons, living or dead, is entirely coincidental.

ALADDIN

An imprint of Simon & Schuster Children's Publishing Division

1230 Avenue of the Americas, New York, New York 10020

First Aladdin hardcover edition October 2019

Text copyright © 2019 by Joan Holub and Suzanne Williams

Jacket illustration copyright © 2019 by Pernille Ørum

Interior illustration of tree copyright © 2019 by Elan Harris

Also available in an Aladdin paperback edition.

All rights reserved, including the right of reproduction in whole or in part in any form.

ALADDIN and related logo are registered trademarks of Simon & Schuster, Inc.

For information about special discounts for bulk purchases, please contact Simon & Schuster Special Sales at 1-866-506-1949 or business@simonandschuster.com.

The Simon & Schuster Speakers Bureau can bring authors to your live event. For more information or to book an event contact the Simon & Schuster Speakers Bureau at 1-866-248-3049 or visit our website at www.simonspeakers.com.

Designed by Laura Lyn DiSiena

The text of this book was set in Baskerville.

Manufactured in the United States of America 0819 FFG

2 4 6 8 10 9 7 5 3 1

Library of Congress Control Number 2019942741

ISBN 978-1-4814-9646-9 (hc)

ISBN 978-1-4814-9645-2 (pbk)

ISBN 978-1-4814-9647-6 (eBook)

For our wonderful readers.

Sloane G., Jeremy G., Andrade Family, Ellis T., Isla W.,
Maia A., Athena H., Ainsley W., Christine D-H., Olive Jean D.,
Eli Reuben D., Lori F., Lily-Ann and Tobi-Dawne S., Kira L.,
Allison B., Jessica W., Sofia W., Kristen S., Olivia C. and
Malia C., Evilynn R., Caitlin R. and Hannah R.,
Madeline W., Layla S., McKenna W.,
and you.

—J. H. and S. W.

Contents

1
Glad Rags

TWELVE-YEAR-OLD IDUN AND HER FRIENDS Freya, Sif, and Skade stomped the snow from their boots as they entered Midgard Mall. "Want to split up to shop at different stores and then meet back here later?" Idun asked the others.

The four girlgoddesses had only just become friends a few weeks ago when they'd all begun attending Asgard Academy and been thrown together as roommates. Principal Odin had invited (ordered, actually) students from all nine worlds of the Norse universe—located on three enormous ring-shaped levels stacked one above the other—to enroll at the newly formed academy.

Skade nodded. "Good idea. I want to check out the boot sales." A half-giant from a second-level world called Jotunheim, she was crazy about boots. The pros and cons of various ski, snow, or high-fashion ones were all Skade had talked about as the girls had walked across the Bifrost Bridge to get to the mall. That tricolor red, blue, and green bridge connected this second-level world of Midgard with the first-level world of Asgard, which was where their academy was located.

"Maybe I'll go with you," Sif told Idun. Sif's golden hair shone brightly in the rays of sun filtering through a skylight overhead. It wasn't real but had been spun from metallic gold threads by two talented dwarfs. "Just to look, though. I've already got two pairs of boots, so I don't really need new ones."

Skade gave her head a shake to dislodge snowflakes.

The motion sent her long white-streaked black hair swaying from side to side. "Need, schmeed. You can *never* have too many boots!"

The other girls laughed. After they all agreed to meet back at the entrance in an hour, Idun whipped out four small snack bags. "Hey, before we split up . . . I brought dried apple chips for everybody."

"Oh, thanks," said Freya, tucking the bag Idun handed her into her pocket.

"Yeah," murmured Skade, quickly pocketing hers, too.

"So thoughtful of you," Sif added a little too brightly.

In fact, as Idun began munching her apple chips (*mmm, nice and chewy*), she noticed that she was the only one doing so.

"Aren't you hungry?" she asked Freya after Skade and Sif headed off.

"I'm saving my chips for later," Freya replied as the two girls started to walk. But Idun noticed her smile seemed a little forced.

Her friends' lack of enthusiasm for the apple chips she'd brought along left Idun feeling a little bummed. She was the girlgoddess of youth, and her magical and deliciously sweet golden apples were what kept all of the academy's goddesses and gods healthy and youthful. Didn't her friends appreciate that?

"So what did you want to shop for? I'm thinking clothes," Freya said, changing the subject. "Although I need more of those like Skade needs more boots!" she added.

Setting aside her hurt feelings, Idun smiled. They both knew Freya already had way more clothes than would fit in her wardrobe back at their room in the girls' dorm. Freya was the most fashion-forward girl at the academy. Though all the girls wore sleeveless wool dresses called *hangerocks* over their simple white linen shifts, hers were always the cutest!

"Skade says you can never have too many boots. Maybe the same could be said about clothes," said Idun.

And apple chips, she thought, but didn't say. "I love your *hangerock,* by the way."

"Thanks! I made it myself." Freya did a quick pose to better display the dark blue *hangerock* she wore beneath her red wool cloak. White snowflakes embroidered around the *hangerock*'s hem sparkled. And fancy tortoiseshell clasps fastened the dress's shoulder straps at the front. Small leather pouches containing intriguing objects dangled from nine bead, seed, or chain necklaces. These were strung between the clasps in a big swoopy smile-shape swag across Freya's chest.

"Everybody sews where I'm from in Vanaheim," Freya went on. "But that doesn't mean I don't like shopping for something someone else made for a change. Plus, it gives me sewing ideas."

As they walked on, Idun gazed ahead to the rows of stores. "I wonder where we should start," she murmured, munching her chips. They were delicious *and* nutritious. It made no sense that her friends hadn't gobbled them up right away. After all, they hadn't eaten any breakfast before coming to the mall. Seemed like they'd be hungry.

"Good question. I'll ask Brising." Freya quickly lifted the coolest of the necklaces she wore—a gorgeous one of hammered gold decorated with small winking jewels. Brising was the name of the shiny walnut-size teardrop-shaped amber jewel dangling from its center. It gave her the power of prophecy.

"Brising, where can we find the best clothes and deals around here?" Freya asked the jewel. Since it always spoke in a low humming sound that only she could understand, Freya listened for a few moments and then repeated aloud what the jewel had said:

> *"Count six doors,*
> *Passing stores.*
> *Find happy rags,*
> *Marked with price tags!"*

"Rags?" echoed Idun. She and Freya looked at each other and burst out laughing.

"Maybe you misunderstood, Brising," Freya told her jewel. "We're shopping for clothes, not rags." She listened for another few moments, then shrugged. "Brising's gone mum."

"Oh well," said Idun. "Let's go past the next six doors and see what we find."

Appearing amused, Freya lifted an eyebrow. "Looking for more appley clothing?"

"Who, me?" Idun asked innocently. "Why would you think that?" With a grin, she patted the gold-colored knit hat she wore over her long brown hair. A brown felt "stem" and green felt leaf were stitched to its top, making the entire hat resemble a gold-colored apple.

Freya eyed the hat. "Uh, maybe because you are ever so slightly apple obsessed?"

Idun grinned. "Maybe so. My apples are important." The apples she tended grew year-round—even in winter snow—in one particular grove in Asgard. Though students often ate them whole, the school's kitchen staff also made them into applesauce and baked goods such as apple turnovers. Or pressed them to make the tasty apple juice served in the school's cafeteria, which was officially called the Valhallateria, or just "the V" for short.

Idun finished her chips and tossed her empty bag into a recycling bin. By now, she and Freya had passed two boot stores, a leather-goods shop, a clock shop, an artisan shop called Wood Goods, and a jewelry store. Suddenly Freya came to a halt. "Cool clothes alert!" she blurted, pointing to a shop across the way. It was called Glad Rags.

"Hey! Brising said '*happy* rags' which is almost the same as 'glad rags.' He must've meant we should try this store," said Idun.

Freya pointed to the motto under the store name on the sign over the door: WE SELL ONE-OF-A-KIND,

GENTLY USED CLOTHING. Smaller print below read: NOW ACCEPTING SECONDHAND CLOTHES FROM GODDESSES, GODS, GIANTS, OR ELVES FOR OUR STOCK.

"Ooh!" Idun said, her face lighting up. "Wouldn't 'one-of-a-kind' describe apple-themed clothes?"

Freya grinned and rolled her eyes merrily. "You, girl, have a one-track mind."

Idun grinned back. Okay, so she definitely *was* a little apple obsessed.

The girls entered the shop. There were numerous racks of clothing inside and just one other customer, who was at the shop's counter. Freya made a beeline for the nearest rack. Expertly she began to flip through its contents. Idun chose the next rack over to search for apple-patterned items.

"Dee-lighted you came shopping here today!" a tiny voice suddenly piped up.

Huh? Idun glanced around. Seeing no one speaking

to her, however, she went back to sorting through the clothing on the rack.

"I looove that necklace!" another similar tiny voice said to Freya. More voices chimed in, agreeing.

"Who said that?" Idun and Freya exclaimed at the same time.

"Maybe the clothes?" Idun ventured.

"Got it in one," said a pink sports jersey bearing a giant white number one on its front.

Each time the girls touched additional items of clothing, they were startled to hear more cheerful voices call out to them.

"Hey! Try me on. I guarantee I'll make you look *purr*fect!" said a shirt with a kitten on its front.

"To wear me is to love me," promised a dress with a heart design.

"So happy you are considering me, even if I am a bit flashy!" squealed a top with tiny lights that blinked on and off when touched.

"I guess they really are *glad* rags," Idun quipped.

"Yes, we're cheerful," a fancy ruffled blouse Freya had pulled out agreed. "Because we're all clothes for special occasions. That's what 'glad rags' means!"

Just then the customer at the counter announced, "Ma'am? I want to make a return." Glancing up, Idun watched the customer shove a large bag across the sales counter. After peeking inside the bag, the curly haired shopkeeper on the other side of the counter raised her eyebrows, which were as bushy as the eyebrows of the customer.

"Humans?" Idun mouthed to Freya. Freya nodded, wiggling her own brows to indicate the reason she thought Idun was probably right. This was Midgard, of course, where humans dwelled, and they all had bushy eyebrows.

"Returns are no problem. I'm Ms. Glad, the store owner," replied the woman behind the counter. Her smile was big and cheery. "I'm so *very* pleased you shop here and only sorry that this time your purchase didn't work out for you."

As Idun listened in on the conversation at the counter, she could also hear the jolly pieces of clothing Freya was rummaging through urging her to try them on and buy them.

"I'll say it didn't work out!" the customer huffed. She pointed to the bag. "There's something downright spooky about that . . . *thing* in there." She lowered her voice so that Idun had to scoot a little closer to hear. "When I put it on last night, it began to tighten around me. And then—and I swear I'm not making this up—it started making these noises. Shrill cries, sort of like seagulls or banshees or something! I took it off at once!"

"A wise move," Ms. Glad said agreeably. She pulled out some coins and handed them over to the woman. "It is never desirable to have one's clothing shriek."

Idun couldn't tell for sure, but it seemed to her that Ms. Glad wasn't at all surprised by what the customer had said. Well, Idun sure was. Clothes that talked cheerfully were one thing. But *shrieking* clothes were quite another. She glanced at the door, wondering if she and Freya should skedaddle.

However, Freya seemed to have not overheard the conversation at the counter. "Ymir's eyeballs! Look at this!" she exclaimed just then.

Ymir was a frost giant who'd lived at the beginning of time. Slain by the gods, his various body parts had been used to grow the nine worlds. And for some reason, everyone spoke of those body parts as slang.

Idun turned toward Freya as her friend held up a bulky bright-orange poncho with short rainbow-colored tassels dangling all over it. Both girls burst out laughing at how ugly it was.

"Yeah, I'm glad Ymir's eyeballs can't see that thing. I sort of wish we couldn't either," said Idun, stepping closer to giggle with Freya over the poncho.

"I can definitely believe this orange poncho is 'one

of a kind' like the sign says," Freya said to Idun. "Who would want to wear something that made them look like a giant pumpkin?"

"HeLLO! I can hear you! And what's wrong with pumpkins?" the poncho demanded to know.

Freya sent Idun an *uh-oh, I forgot it could hear us* look. "Do clothes have feelings?" she whispered to Idun.

"Not sure," Idun whispered back. "I would've guessed 'glad' rags could only feel gladness, but that poncho sounds annoyed. Makes sense the owner wouldn't want to call her store 'Annoyed Rags,' though."

The girls giggled, but then quickly stopped when they noticed that the poncho seemed to wilt. "Not everyone has the same taste in clothes," Idun reminded it in a kind voice.

Catching on, Freya added, "Right. I'm sure plenty of people are dying for an orange poncho with tassels. If they knew you were in here, they'd be rushing in to buy you."

The poncho turned a happier, brighter shade of orange. "Yes, of course!" it said, all cheery again.

"Do you girls need help finding anything?" Ms. Glad called out after the customer who'd been at the counter hurried out the shop's door empty-handed.

Idun hoped Ms. Glad hadn't overheard her and Freya. What if she thought they were making fun of the clothes in her shop? They weren't! Well, except for the orange poncho, maybe.

"Thanks, but we're okay for now," Freya replied as she started to flip through the clothes on another rack.

"Sorry about the small rip in my seam!" an item called out merrily when she touched it. "A giant tried me on and then accidently shape-shifted herself larger. It'd be an easy repair, though!"

Keeping half an eye on Freya, Idun worked her way closer to the counter, her gaze mostly on that customer's returned bag. The comments she'd overheard had left her super curious about its contents. As she edged toward the bag, she did a quick search of two more racks but found no apple-patterned items.

"Um, actually," Idun said to the owner when she neared the counter, "can I see what's in the bag that other customer just returned?"

The owner raised an eyebrow. "If you dare." But then she laughed as if she were only joking.

Or is she? Idun wondered.

Still smiling, Ms. Glad opened the bag and carefully lifted out a cloak. Wow! It was glorious, covered in gleaming horizontally striped brown and white feathers. When she gently shook it out, Idun felt her heart quicken. Though she couldn't have said just why, especially since the cloak was not apple-themed, she immediately wanted it. She reached out to stroke its white-tipped feathers. As soon as she touched them, the cloak spoke up.

"Fly away with me!" it urged her. "We'll be birds of a feather that stick together."

Idun grinned, and that 'wanting' feeling intensified.

Who cared if the customer who'd returned it had called it "spooky"? Idun had to have it!

"Fabulous, isn't it?" Ms. Glad said enthusiastically. "Those are falcon feathers, by the way."

"Interesting," said Idun. She reached out, dying to try it on.

Suddenly Freya appeared beside them. "What an unusual cloak," she said, peering down at it.

Unusual as in weird? Idun wondered, suddenly unsure of her own fashion sense.

But then Freya said, "It's quirky, but cool. Look how well made it is. The feathers all line up so that the horizontal bands of color match perfectly." She smiled at Idun. "Definitely one of a kind. And in a good way."

"So you like it?" Idun asked, still a little unsure.

Freya nodded. "Definitely."

"Enough to buy?" Idun pressed. She really wanted the cloak, but she'd like fashion-forward Freya's seal of approval first.

"Maybe," said Freya. She turned toward the shop owner. "How much is it?"

"I can offer it at a very low price," Ms. Glad told her. "Because as wonderful as this cloak is, it's been returned to my shop three times already. I'd really like to see it go to a good home. So if you'll agree to take it on a no-refunds, no-exchanges basis, I'll cut the price in half. You can have it for a hundred kroner."

Freya's pale-blue eyes lit up. "Fantastic!" she said excitedly. "That's a bargain. I'll take it!"

Wha—? Idun's face fell. Too late, she realized that she hadn't made it clear that *she* was interested in buying the cloak.

"Hey, thanks for finding it for me," Freya said to Idun as she fished in the pocket of her *hangerock* for coins.

When Idun said nothing, Freya glanced up at her. Confusion came into her eyes as she noticed the crestfallen look on Idun's face. "Wait a minute," she said.

"Did I make a mistake here? Do you want the cloak?"

Idun hesitated. As much as she did want the falcon feather cloak, she could see that Freya wanted it too. She prided herself on her generosity. It would feel selfish to take the cloak for herself, even if she had seen it first. They hadn't known each other all that long, and she really wanted Freya to like her. It might help seal their new friendship if Idun let her have the cloak.

"Well, I do like it. But you called dibs first. That cloak will look great on you." In the back of her mind she somehow expected Freya to guess how she really felt and say, *No, you should have it.*

Instead, Freya beamed at her. "Really? That's so sweet of you!" She handed over the coins to Ms. Glad.

Upset, but not knowing what to do about it, Idun moved away from the counter as Freya completed her purchase. Turning, she headed for the door, hoping Freya wouldn't guess how unhappy she was. When Idun bumped a sweater with a crystal ball pictured on its front, it happily singsonged a prediction: "Do a good deed, and you'll get what you need."

"Oh, hush," Idun scolded it. "I did do a good deed, and now *Freya* has what I need!"

"Do a good deed, and you'll get what you need," the sweater repeated cheerily. Idun just rolled her eyes. She felt grumpy and somehow cheated out of that cloak, though she knew it wasn't really fair of her to think that.

Moments later, the two girls exited the shop. "I feel bad that you didn't find anything to buy," Freya said, bagged cloak in hand. "We still have time to check out at least one more shop before we meet up with Skade and Sif if you want."

"No, that's okay," Idun replied in as bright a voice as she could manage. She'd lost her chance to own the feather cloak. Nothing else would seem quite as wonderful, even something apple-themed.

That store had been named incorrectly, she decided as they walked away from it. It should've been named Sad Rags or Mad Rags. Because that's how she'd wound up feeling after shopping in there!

2
On the Bridge

WHEN IDUN, FREYA, SKADE, AND SIF FINALLY met up again a few minutes later, Idun noticed somewhat glumly that she was the only one not carrying a shopping bag.

"Do you guys want to walk back to the academy, or should we take my cart?" Freya asked. Her fingers played with the strings of one of the pouches that dangled from her necklaces. Inside that particular pouch was a magical cat's-eye marble. Simply by tossing the marble in the

air, she could make it transform into a red cart pulled by two large tabby cats that was big enough to zoom all four of the girls through the air!

Freya sounded lighthearted and jolly. *Sure, why wouldn't she?* Idun thought enviously. *She has a great new cloak!*

"Your kittycart would make the trip shorter," said Sif as the girls left the mall. She glanced up at the mostly blue sky and took a deep breath. The air she exhaled was frosty. "But I vote we walk back. It's a nice day."

"Yeah, cold and crisp, just the way I like it," said Skade. Pulling on her mittens, she peered up at the sky too. Though a half foot of snow covered the groun no new snow was falling. "I vote for walking. Sif I can try out our new snow boots!" She held u shopping bag.

"Okay with me," Freya agreed.

"Me too," said Idun. She pointed to t carried. "So you bought a pair after all?"

Sif nodded sheepishly. "Skade's enth

is contagious. I gave in to temptation." She and Skade sat down on a wooden bench just outside the mall to put on their new boots.

"Ooh, what a great shade of purple!" Freya exclaimed when Skade pulled hers from her bag.

"Isn't it?" Skade said, admiring her purchase. "According to the sales clerk, they're plum-violet." She pulled off the green pair of boots she'd been wearing and placed them in her bag. Then she pulled on her new ones.

Sif's new boots were a sparkly gold color that matched her waist-long golden hair. "They're beautiful," Idun told her. "I can see why you were tempted."

Sif smiled, looking pleased at the compliment.

Idun was surprised when Freya didn't show Sif and Skade her falcon feather cloak. But then again, the other two girls were so excited about their new boots that they hadn't asked what was in her bag. Whenever Freya did decide to show them, Idun hoped she wasn't

24

around. Because she didn't think she could bear to hear Freya's enthusiasm for the cloak. Her happiness would make Idun feel that much worse about not getting the cloak herself!

The four friends tromped across the snow-covered ground in front of the mall to a small ramp that led onto the Bifrost Bridge. Some called the huge, gleaming arch the *rainbow* bridge, but since it was only made up of three colors, it wasn't actually a complete rainbow. The people of Asgard—they were called the *Aesir*—had built the bridge out of fire, air, and water. Red for fire, blue for air, and green for water.

"Ow! Just a sec," said Sif, starting to hobble. "Rock in my boot." Plunking down on a knee-high boulder, she began unlacing the boot.

At the bottom of the on-ramp to the bridge was a small sign. "'Beware of trolls,'" Freya said, reading it aloud. She glanced at her friends. "You know how trolls supposedly like to hang out under bridges and threaten anyone who tries to cross? I actually saw some once, on my way to the academy our first day of school. They were just jumping around on the ramp, laughing and having fun. Not being scary at all."

"I've heard stepping on this bridge gives trolls a hot foot, even though it feels cold to the touch," said Sif. "Giants, too. Because they both go barefoot all the time. Its heat is what keeps them from crossing over and sneaking into Asgard."

"The bridge hasn't ever bothered me," said Skade, "maybe because I'm only *half*-giant. Plus, I wear boots."

"You know, sometimes I wonder if trolls have just gotten a bad rap," mused Idun. "Maybe it's unfair to think we should beware of them."

Skade grinned and then cupped her hands around her mouth. "Listen up, you trolls!" she yelled. "We're not afraid of you. Come out, come out, wherever you are!"

"Shhh!" the other three girls hissed. Unlike Freya, Idun had never seen a troll, and she wasn't sure she ever wanted to until they knew for sure that they weren't scary. When no trolls appeared—scary *or* friendly—the four girls all laughed in relief.

"Ready," Sif announced. Having emptied the rock from her boot and re-laced it, she hopped up and the girls moved on.

Just beyond the BEWARE OF TROLLS sign was a large map. It showed how the nine worlds all fit together under an enormous ash tree called Yggdrasil (also known as the World Tree). Idun had the map memorized. Still, she paused to study it.

The gigantic tree was at the map's center with three fat rings encircling its trunk, spaced one above the other. There were three worlds on each of the three rings.

The first ring—the top one—included Asgard (world of the Aesir, where Idun and Sif had grown up), Vanaheim (world of the Vanir, where Freya and her brother, Frey, had come from), and Alfheim (world of the light-elves, many of whom attended the academy).

The second ring—the one in the middle—included Midgard (world of the humans), Jotunheim (world of the frost giants, where Skade had come from), and Darkalfheim (world of the dwarfs, an underground labyrinth of tunnels and caves).

The third ring—the bottom one—included Niflheim (world of ice and fog and home to the dead), Helheim (world also inhabited by the dead that was ruled by a hideous female monster), and Muspelheim (world of the fire giants).

Sif gave a dramatic shudder as she, Freya, and Skade passed by Idun and the map. "Ooh, just thinking about the third ring always gives me the willies."

"Me too," Idun agreed. Then she gasped as a short, squat creature suddenly appeared to join her in staring at the map. It reached out with its stubby fingers to trace the illustrated paths of Yggdrasil's three enormous roots. One root was planted in each of the three rings at the site of a spring or well that nourished the tree.

Yggdrasil's health was just as important as the health of the special apple grove Idun tended. *More* important, really. Because the future of all worlds hung on the enormous tree's welfare. Besides providing a link between the three rings, Yggdrasil sheltered the worlds from storms, supplied wood for building, provided a home for animals, and much, much more.

"Can I help you find your way?" Idun asked the creature kindly. Yggdrasil was super huge—some said it could take a lifetime to walk all the way around it. It was easy to get lost in unfamiliar parts of the worlds.

The creature whipped around to stare at her with its tiny eyes. It had a huge warty nose and skin that looked as rough as tree bark. "I've already found what I was looking for!" it crowed. "Four tasty students! Ringy-ding-ding! And rooty-toot-toots! I'll grind your bones and steal your boots!"

Idun froze in fear. Up ahead, her friends had over-heard. They looked back over their shoulders.

"Troll!" Freya yelled to Idun. "Not a friendly one! Run!"

Idun took off. *Stomp! Stomp! Stomp!* As all four girls clattered over the bridge, the troll cackled and chased after them.

"*Faster!* It's gaining on us!" yelled Sif.

When the others sped up, so did Idun. Soon she'd caught up to them.

"Wait a second," Skade said, after they'd put some distance between themselves and the creature. "Is that troll wearing shoes?"

"You're right," said Sif, glancing back at it. "It is!"

Idun dared to look back too. "*Yellow* shoes," she added.

The four girls came to a dead halt. They looked at one another, their breaths heaving their chests. "Loki!" they exclaimed.

Laughter echoed behind them as the "troll" shape-shifted into one of their fellow classmates, the boygod

Loki. He'd tricked them just to give them a scare! His yellow shoes were the tip-off, though. They were magic and allowed him to race like the wind, skimming over land and water. And that's what he did now, zooming past them on the bridge toward the academy, laughing all the way.

"Fooled you!" he yelled back at them.

"That guy is sooo annoying! Always making trouble," said Sif.

"Yeah, I scuffed my new boots because of him," Skade complained as they followed Loki across the bridge.

"Gosh, if only you had others back at the dorm to change into," Freya teased lightly, making everyone grin.

"You must have . . . what . . . a dozen pairs by now?" asked Idun.

Skade cocked her head, considering the question. Finally, she said, "Counting my new pair, thirteen. Each is special in its own way, though." She pointed down at her new ones. "I bought these mainly for their color. But I also have speedy boots, lightweight boots, knee-highs, shorties, fur-lined, and so on."

Sif scrunched her nose. "Isn't thirteen an unlucky number?"

Freya nodded in agreement. "You should cut back to nine pairs," she told Skade as she touched the necklaces that hung in a swag across her chest. "I always wear exactly nine necklaces."

Really? thought Idun. She'd never realized that. Made sense, though. As everyone knew, nine was a super lucky number because it matched the number of worlds in the Norse universe.

"Or I could just find one stray boot to add to my collection," said Skade.

"What?" Idun, Freya, and Sif chorused.

Skade grinned. "Thirteen pairs equals twenty-six boots, right? Add one more boot and that makes twenty-seven.

And twenty-seven is *three times* the lucky number nine!"

As the girls all laughed at her math logic, Skade suddenly pointed at the bag Freya was carrying. "Hey, what'd you buy?"

"Ooh! Wait till you see. Prepare to be amazed," Freya said, her eyes twinkling. She stopped on the bridge to open her bag.

Idun tensed.

Sif sent her a sideways glance. "No bag for you?"

"Nuh-uh," Idun said with a shrug. "Didn't find anything I wanted." It was a lie of course. Trying not to feel *too* resentful, she watched Freya pull the falcon feather cloak from her bag.

"Ta-da!" said Freya.

"Hooray! It's a great flying day," said the cloak in its "glad" voice. "Put me on and let's hit the skies!"

"Wow!" Skade exclaimed. "A talking cloak! Do like it said. Put it on."

Idun shifted from one foot to the other. If only she had told Freya she wanted to buy the cloak back in the shop. Was it too late?

"Wait! Where did you get it?" Sif asked Freya, eyeing the cloak suspiciously. "Are you sure it's safe to wear?"

"Sure. Don't worry." As Freya explained about the talking clothes back in the Glad Rags shop, Skade and Sif examined and admired the cloak.

Idun looked on, jealous. That cloak should have been hers! "A lady was returning it. She said it shrieked!" she blurted out.

Freya cocked her head at Idun. "Really? You didn't tell me that before."

Instantly Idun felt guilty for trying to ruin Freya's excitement. To make up for it, she added, "I'm sure it's fine. That nice shop lady wouldn't have resold it to you if it wasn't. Here, I'll hold your other cloak for you while you put on the new one."

"Thanks," Freya said with a grateful smile. She

slipped off her red cloak and handed it to Idun along with her bag. Whipping her arms, she swirled the feather cloak over her shoulders. No sooner had she done this than something amazing happened. The new cloak tightened around her. Wings opened up from its sides.

Flap! Flap! Freya took to the sky, her legs and booted feet becoming claws, and her head becoming that of a falcon with a sharp hooked beak.

Openmouthed in surprise, Idun, Skade, and Sif stared upward as falcon-Freya made several awkward, jerky circles overhead. "EeYEE! EeYEE!"

"You okay up there?" called Sif.

"Freya! Get back down here!" Skade yelled. "You've never shape-shifted before. It's too dangerous."

However, as Freya flew overhead, her circles became smoother. Her high-pitched "caws" grew calmer. She even executed a barrel roll!

"She's really getting the hang of flying!" said Sif, sounding impressed.

"EeYEE! EeYEE!" cried falcon-Freya.

"Those caws must be the 'shrieking' the lady who'd returned the cloak was talking about back in the store," Idun said, thinking aloud.

Suddenly Freya zoomed in to land on the bridge a short distance ahead of the girls. While the girls ran toward her, she managed to shrug off the cloak. Instantly she returned to her girlgoddess form.

"Ymir's elbows!" Skade exclaimed as she, Idun, and Sif gathered around Freya. "I can't believe you found a shape-shifting cloak. They're super rare!" She picked up the cloak, which had landed on the bridge. Before handing it back to Freya, she gave its feathers an admiring stroke.

Shape-shifting cloak? thought Idun, going pale. *I've given up a rare shape-shifting cloak?* Envy pricked her again, and panic over her mistake swelled inside her. Freya would never give the cloak to her now! Plus, she'd sound like sour apples if she even asked her to.

Freya was beaming. "Cloaks like this one *are* rare." She folded it neatly over her arm, her fingers straightening its feathers.

"Rare," the cloak echoed happily.

Clearly, you had to be *wearing* the special cloak to activate its transformational magic. Maybe it wasn't too late. What if Idun grabbed it and put it on now herself? Would it switch its loyalty to her?

"I wonder if its powers would work for anyone wearing it," said Sif, practically reading her mind.

"Obeya only Freya," the cloak singsonged.

This made Freya laugh merrily. Quick as a wink, she bagged her feather cloak and put on her red wool one.

Frustration filled Idun anew. How had a morning that had started off so well ended up so crummy?

As they started walking again, Freya leaned over and gave Idun a quick hug. "It's thanks to Idun that I got the cloak. She's the one who pointed it out to me."

"Did you guess it was a shape-shifting cloak?" Sif asked Idun.

"No," Idun admitted dully. "The shopkeeper didn't mention that."

"I bet she didn't know," Freya added. "She was a human Midgardian, and they can't shape-shift. It probably didn't even occur to her that the cloak could be something really special."

Skade cocked her head. "But you said her shop was full of talking clothes. That's pretty special right there."

"The shop's sign said she accepted secondhand clothes from goddesses, gods, giants, or elves," said Idun. "Maybe a giant or goddess customer helped her out by casting a talking spell over her stock. I'm guessing that whoever gave her that cloak had no idea it was a shape-shifting one."

Sif nodded. "Yeah, if they'd known, they would've *kept* it."

"And if the shopkeeper knew, she wouldn't have sold it to me so cheap," Freya said.

Skade's eyes lit up. "So you got it at a discount?"

"Fifty percent off," Freya told her proudly.

"Wow!" Skade, queen of the sales, looked impressed. "I wonder if she sells used ski boots."

"Hey, there's Heimdall," said Sif. She nodded ahead toward the end of the bridge where the exceedingly tall, broad-shouldered, gold-toothed, pointy-bearded Asgard Academy security guard stood. Dressed in uniform, he carried an enormous sword at his side.

Idun eyed the huge horn that was slung across his shoulder by a leather strap. It was shaped like a ram's horn and made of polished gold. Whenever Heimdall blew on it to mark the beginnings and endings of mealtimes and classes, the sound was extremely loud.

"Who's that talking to him?" Idun wondered, pointing at two boys standing with their backs toward the girls.

"Black hair and . . . *yellow shoes*? One of them is that

fake-troll boygod, Loki!" sputtered Skade. Just then Loki rose in his magic shoes to hover a few inches above the ground before lowering again.

"Typical," said Sif. "First he scares us half to death. Then he hangs around at the end of the bridge like he didn't do anything wrong and we have no reason to be mad."

"I think he's forgotten all about us. Let's sneak up and give him a scare this time," suggested Freya.

Since Heimdall was concentrating on whatever the boys were saying and the boys' backs were still turned away from the girls, none of the three noticed the girls' approach.

Cool. Idun was curious to overhear what they were talking about.

"So exactly how long does it take to grow a beard like yours?" the boy with Loki was asking Heimdall. Noting his curly brown hair, Idun decided it must be their classmate Bragi.

The four girls grinned at one another. So this was

the sort of stuff boys talked about when no girls were around?

"And when did you get whiskers? Like, how old were you when you grew some, I mean?" they heard Loki ask the guard.

Before Heimdall could reply, Bragi butted in. "Is there a way to grow your beard a certain color?" he asked. "Think I could grow a gray one like Odin's? That would be awesome! I could braid it and maybe keep a bird's nest in there."

The girls stifled giggles. Picturing Loki and Bragi with beards was a funny idea. Especially bird's nest beards!

Heimdall lifted an eyebrow at the boys. "I wouldn't be in such a big hurry to grow up if I were you." Known for his keen eyesight and hearing, but not for his sense of humor, he added, "Grown-ups have to shoulder lots of responsibilities that I don't think you're ready for."

Neither boygod need worry about facing those "responsibilities," Idun thought as the girls crept closer.

As long as they kept eating her golden apples of youth, they'd never grow old.

Unfortunately, Heimdall caught sight of Idun and her friends before they could give Loki a scare. "Thunder Girls!" he boomed in his usual loud way. He'd given them that nickname when they'd first started at the academy because he'd been irritated at the thundering sounds their snow boots made when they raced over the bridge.

Far from feeling offended, however, the girls had decided they liked the nickname. Thunder was power-ful, after all, so it indicated they had girl power! They'd even chosen "Thunder Girls" as their group's name and written it on a cute sign that they'd hung on the door of the room they shared in the girls' dorm.

Loki must have realized that the girls had overheard him and Bragi talking to Heimdall. His face went pink with embarrassment, and his dark-blue eyes flitted down-ward for a moment. He recovered quickly, however. "Move along, *Blunder* Girls. This is guy talk. So unless

42

you're planning to shape-shift into guys, just keep on walking. Oh, wait, I just remembered that none of you except Sif can shape-shift. And she can't do it very well!"

"Grr," growled Sif. But it was true that her shape-shifting skills were limited. She could only become a swan or a tree. That was all.

Over her shoulder, Freya murmured to the other three girls. "If he only knew."

"If he only knew what?" asked Heimdall. You couldn't sneak any whispers past this guy. Not with his super-keen hearing! And when Freya wrapped her arms around the bag containing her new cloak, his shrewd gaze moved to it. "What have you got there, Thunder Girl?"

"Oh, nothing. I just bought a new cloak," said Freya.

"A shape-shifting one," Skade boasted.

Instantly the boys' attention became riveted on the girls. "Yeah, right," scoffed Loki.

"'Yeah, right' is right," blurted Freya, unable to let his put-down pass. "My cloak will help me chase after anyone who plays tricks on us from now on. Tricks like pretending to be a troll."

"Or stealing apples," added Idun. She was referring to something that had happened a while back, when Loki had shape-shifted into an eagle and stolen one of her precious apples of youth while she was picking them in her special grove. Of course, if the feathered cloak were *hers*, she could chase him off *herself* if he ever tried that again!

Heimdall plunked his fists at his hips and demanded, "What's this about shape-shifting?"

Bragi reached for his lyre, which was strung over one shoulder. Hazel eyes twinkling, he strummed it. Then he began to sing softly.

"Girls crossing the Bifrost on their homeward walk
Are making us curious with shape-shifting talk."

He finished with a flourish of his fingers across the strings and then grinned at Idun for some unknown reason.

When she automatically smiled back, he perked up, looking pleased. It almost seemed like he'd sung his song hoping to make her do just that! *But why would he?* she wondered.

She only knew Bragi a little. He was in a couple of her classes. Clever with words, he was known to practice new songs while walking in the forest. She'd often heard him while she was picking her apples.

Loki was eyeing Freya's bag. "So you've got a shape-shifting cloak in there?"

"Yep. I bought it at Midgard Mall," Freya told him matter-of-factly.

A look of dismay flitted across Loki's face. But then it was replaced by his trademark smirk. "You found a shape-shifting cloak in a shop at the mall? I don't think so. If you really have one, prove it. Let's see it work."

Freya jutted out her chin. "Sure, no problem!"

Uh-oh, thought Idun. Everyone knew Loki was the best shape-shifter at Asgard Academy. And he liked it that way. What would he do when he saw how powerful

Freya's new cloak was? Would he try to steal it, like he had Freya's necklace and Idun's apples not long ago? Loki had a reputation as a troublemaker at the academy. One that was well deserved!

Still, despite the tricks he'd played on her and others, Idun was convinced there must be *some* goodness in him. No one could be all bad, right? Maybe, like with trolls, his bad rap wasn't necessarily fair.

Suddenly the words spoken by the sweater with the crystal ball image on it in the mall came back to her: "Do a good deed, and you'll get what you need." If she could somehow help keep Loki out of trouble, that might allow him to improve his reputation. And that would be a good deed indeed. One that would benefit him and everyone at AA! But how this deed would help her get what *she* needed—namely, the feather cloak—she wasn't sure.

Before she could give this more thought, they all heard a familiar sound.

3
A Plan Hatches

***T*OOOT!**

Freya had been reaching for her new cloak, probably intent on proving its powers, when Heimdall lifted his horn to his lips. Now her hands flew to cover her ears instead.

Idun and the others covered their ears too. The blast signaling that lunch would be over in fifteen minutes was so loud that Idun could almost feel her brain rattle around inside her skull. Everyone took their hands from their ears as Heimdall lowered his horn, and Bragi exclaimed: "I would swear on old Ymir's hat that even Nidhogg just heard *that*!"

"Heard it from way down on the third ring?" Loki scoffed. "Doubt it." Nidhogg was a dragon that dwelled in the third ring's dark, foggy world of Niflheim, where he gnawed on Yggdrasil's third and lowest root.

At Loki's unkind comment, Bragi's face fell a little.

To make Bragi feel less embarrassed, Idun smiled at him, saying, "So you think Ymir wore a hat?"

"Sure. It's cold in Jotunheim," Bragi replied, perking up. "And if Ymir's hat was a wool one, that's probably where sheep came from!"

Everyone (except the solemn Heimdall) laughed at this, even Loki. Long ago, the giant Ymir's bones had become mountains; his hair, trees; his skull, the sky. Even his eyelashes became a wall that encircled the human world of Midgard. Who knew? Bragi's woolly sheep guess could be right!

Suddenly Skade's stomach rumbled loudly. "I'm starving!" she exclaimed.

"Me too," chorused Freya and Sif.

Idun shot them a surprised glance. "Really? Didn't you eat your apple snacks?" She'd finished hers back at the mall. So although she was hungry again, she wasn't starving.

"Oh, um, sure. Shopping makes you hungry, that's all," said Skade. But she didn't quite look at Idun as she said this.

Was Skade lying? wondered Idun. She had a feeling her roomies hadn't eaten or appreciated her apple snacks at all, and that hurt.

"Same as you, I'm hungry too!" Bragi rhymed. "I played Spydkast with some of the guys all morning." Spydkast was a competition that involved running and then throwing a spear as far as one could. Slipping back into rhyme, he added, "It was tons of fun. But as usual, Thor won."

Red-haired Thor was the biggest and strongest boygod in the entire school. He had a short-handled hammer named Mjollnir, which always returned to his hand no matter how far he threw it. With the help of that hammer, Thor had led the effort to keep frost giants and other enemies from getting through the wall around Asgard.

"Yeah, I was kind of busy myself," said Loki, smirking. "*Troll*ing for fun, you might say."

Before the girls could respond to his taunt, Heimdall warned, "Better get a move on or you won't make it to lunch before the Valhallateria closes."

A moment later Heimdall ushered the two boys and four girls to stand before a pair of gold doors. These hovered in midair without visible support at the end of the bridge. The doors were actually a magical portal. It was the quickest route to the academy, whose many buildings were scattered among Yggdrasil's humongous lofty branches high above Asgard's villages and towns.

With a last glance at the boys, Heimdall surprised them with a wink and a rhyme of his own: "And don't go growing a beard, 'cause you'll look very weird!"

Hmm. Maybe the security guard had a better sense of humor than anyone credited him with, thought Idun.

Once through the portal, the six students were abruptly whisked away! Idun's long brown hair and skirts whipped wildly as she was whooshed with the others through a lengthy vine tunnel. The giant hollowed-out vine was big enough to walk (or whoosh) through. Seconds later, they all tumbled to land high in Yggdrasil, upon a branch that was so wide you couldn't see from one side of it to the other. Entire forests of trees way smaller than Yggdrasil, plus various flora and fauna, thrived upon this branch and many more like it.

Pushing her hair out of her eyes, Idun saw that Sif, Skade, and Freya had landed on their hands and knees about ten yards behind her. Loki and Bragi had wound up ahead of all of them.

Idun had somehow managed to land on her feet. But her legs had gotten tangled in her skirt while she'd whirled through the vine tunnel. When she tried to untangle herself now, she lost her balance and fell backward onto a snowbank.

"Whoa!" she called out. She was trying to push herself to stand when Bragi came over to help. She grabbed his hand. "Thanks . . . uh-oh . . . oh no!" She slipped, accidentally pulling him down onto the snowbank too.

"Sorry!" she told him. She tried to scramble to her feet on her own and so did he. But after slipping and sliding, both fell back in the snow. *Thump!* When they tried again, they bumped heads. Idun reached both arms toward him. "How about if we hold hands, but lean away from each other while we push up with our feet?" she suggested.

Bragi nodded, grabbing her hands. "I'm a fan of that plan!"

And it worked! Once they were both standing up

52

again, it suddenly dawned on Idun that she was holding hands with a boy for the very first time. Immediately she yanked her hands away and took a step backward. Her face burned with embarrassment. "Uh . . . thanks," she mumbled. Glancing around nervously, she noticed the sparkling gold-thatched roof up ahead through Yggdrasil's branches. The Valhallateria.

"Sure. No problem." Bragi seemed unruffled, his hazel eyes sparkling. Making no attempt to rhyme this time, he said with a grin, "If you ever need someone to stop you from standing up in snow again, I'm at your service."

Idun giggled.

Bragi's grin widened. He stooped to pick up the apple-hat she hadn't realized she'd dropped, and handed it to her. "I am sometimes clumsy and must confess, I don't often rescue damsels in distress."

Loki overheard this last remark as he tromped through the snow to join them. He rolled his eyes at

Bragi. "Give the corny rhymes a rest, dude. She rescued *you*. She's not some damsel in distress." Then he grinned. "But maybe she's the apple of your eye?"

It was an obvious reference to her goddess role as keeper of the apples of youth, Idun knew. But was Loki also hinting what she thought he was hinting?

She looked over at Bragi. Maybe so! A blush as red as an apple (only not Idun's magic ones, which were all golden) was stealing over his face. "I . . . um . . . I . . . ," he stuttered. It was the first time Idun had ever seen the talkative boy at a loss for words. Bragi's talkativeness was one of the things she liked about him. He was always in a good mood and usually seemed to have no trouble coming up with stuff to say.

"Oh, get over yourself," Loki told him, bumping his shoulder lightly with a fist. "I was just joking."

"Let's get going before we miss lunch," urged Skade, as the other three girls caught up to Idun and the two boys.

"Here's an idea," Loki said to Freya as all six of them hurried toward the Valhallateria. "For once I'm not all that hungry. So why don't you let me try out this so-called shape-shifting cloak while the rest of you eat?"

Freya arched an eyebrow. "Sure. Just trade me your yellow shoes at the same time."

"Whaaa?" said Loki, taken aback. "No way."

"Ditto," said Freya. "The cloak is too precious to share, just like your shoes. Got it?"

"Oh, all right," Loki grumbled. "Promise you'll show me what the cloak can do after lunch, though? Pretty please?" Then he grinned. It was an endearing grin. One that constantly helped him get out of trouble and also get what he wanted.

"I guess," Freya said reluctantly. She probably only gave in because she knew Loki wouldn't give up until he'd seen her cloak in action. Or maybe it was that tricky grin of his.

When they reached the Valhallateria, Bragi pulled

on one of its V-shaped door handles and then held the door open to let the others enter first.

Loki grinned. "You're such a gentleman," he teased as he sped through the door ahead of the girls.

Freya rolled her eyes as they followed Loki inside. "That's something no one would ever accuse Loki of being."

"Isn't that the truth," agreed Skade.

"Thanks, Bragi," Idun called over her shoulder after moving inside. Catching his eye, she smiled at him. Loki shouldn't have teased him about being a gentleman. If she'd gotten to the door first, she would've held it open too, same as Bragi. Good manners were . . . well . . . *good*!

They were so late by now that most of the V's tables were either empty or being cleared off. Skade and Sif dropped their shopping bags on a nearby table. Freya hung on to hers. Probably a good idea with that sneaky Loki being so interested in her cloak. Luckily, he'd sat down at a table across the room. And now Bragi was crossing the V to join him.

"Drinks! Quick!" yelled Sif. They all knew the rule. You could still get served a meal as long as you were seated with a beverage in hand before Heimdall's end-of-lunch toot blared.

The four girls immediately rushed for Heidrun, the larger-than-life ceramic goat fountain. It stood in the middle of the room upon a flat, rectangular tabletop formed from green-painted "leaves." A great pedestal shaped like a stout tree trunk supported the tabletop itself. After grabbing green glass *hrimkalders*—short cups with rounded bottoms—they filled them with sparkly apple juice that poured out of spigots on all sides of the ceramic goat.

Back at their table again, Freya, Skade, and Sif stashed their bags under their chairs. All had legs made from bent metal spears, with backs and seats made from thick wooden shields set at right angles.

"Phew! Made it!" Sif exclaimed as Heimdall's horn announced the end of lunch service. However, just then, a pear zoomed through the air past the girls' noses.

"Uh-oh." Freya hunched her shoulders. "The downside of coming late to lunch is about to begin."

The girls' gazes flew to the carved wooden friezes that covered all four of the Valhallateria's walls. Painted in blues, yellows, greens, reds, and other bright colors, the sculpted friezes were filled with scenes of heroic warriors who were mostly feasting or marching. Although these warriors usually stood still like figures in any normal painting, they sometimes began to actually move. And fight.

"Attaaack!" With resounding battle cries, sculpted warriors hurled food across the room at foes on opposite walls. They grabbed turnips, carrots, potatoes, apples, bread rolls, and whatever else they found for ammo within their paintings.

Whoosh! A turnip whizzed over the girls' heads. They

ducked just in time and it continued on to the opposite frieze, and whacked a warrior on the shoulder. *Thwack!*

Returning fire, that warrior threw a potato at the turnip-tossing warrior on the opposite wall. *Thump!* "How do you like them taters?" he yelled when the potato found its target.

These daily end-of-meal battles were basically funny food fights. But to the heroes in the paintings, this was war! They taunted one another. "Take that! And that! Losers! Na-na-na-na-nah!"

Meanwhile, Valkyries that worked as servers during meals zoomed around the Valhallateria, their booted feet hovering inches above the floor. One of them rushed up to the girls' table now, balancing a six-foot-wide tray of meals atop the palm of her hand.

Even as the bombardment ramped up around her, she managed to calmly hand out plates containing salad, strawberries, and open-faced meat-and-cheese sandwiches. With a flick of her wrist, she pulled spoons, knives, and rolled-up napkins from rows of loops down the sash across her chest and passed those out too.

Skilled at avoiding flying food, she kept an eye out and flapped her wings to swoop and dive out of harm's way now and then. However, she couldn't see everything. *Thonk!* A large, ripe plum suddenly splatted and smooshed against the carved *V* on the front of her gleaming metal helmet. Tall wings on either side of the helmet quickly bent to brush the resulting goo away like windshield wipers.

"There's a reason we wear these helmets," she quipped cheerily before she zoomed back toward the kitchen to reload her tray.

"Look out!" yelled Skade.

Idun and the others ducked as a volley of bread rolls went sailing in an arc overhead. Though these food battles were a bit aggravating, they were nothing like the *real* battles that had once taken place during a war between Asgard and Vanaheim. It was because of that devastating war that Odin had recently established Asgard Academy, with the goal of improving relations among the nine different worlds. As part of his plan, he'd brought Idun and other students here to this school. He was hoping they'd set a good example for all nine worlds in learning to get along.

To encourage his goal, students were required to sit with students they didn't normally hang out with for at least one meal per day in the Valhallateria. Which meant that Idun and her three friends would all sit apart at dinner, since they'd chosen to sit together now.

Looking a bit concerned, Freya scooted her shopping bag farther under her chair so it wouldn't get food-bombed. "I wish I hadn't told Loki about my shape-shifting cloak," she fretted as she took a sip of apple juice from her *hrimkalder*.

"Too late now," said Skade. Calmly she jerked her head to one side as a carrot flew past her ear. Then she took a big bite of her open-faced sandwich.

Freya nodded glumly. "Yeah, that cat—er, *cloak*—is already out of the bag."

"Loki would have found out sooner or later anyway," Sif pointed out. When a plump strawberry lobbed from a frieze dropped into her lap, she picked it up and popped it into her mouth. "Mm-mm."

"Yeah. Impossible to keep a cloak that cool a secret for long. Unless you never wear it," Idun commented to Freya.

"But whah wuh be the fun of that?" protested Skade, talking around another bite of sandwich.

"True," Freya said. "It's going to get lots of flying time with me—" Her words broke off as a hail of hazelnuts rained down onto the girls' table.

"This is nuts!" Idun heard the cloak murmur. Freya reached under her chair and into her bag to stroke its feathers.

Just then, some girlgiants walked by with apple juice refills, smirking as they passed Idun and her friends.

Although these students could transform to become giant-size whenever they wanted, right now they were regular girl–size.

Suddenly the girlgiants pretended to sneeze. But instead of going *Achoo! Achoo!* they went, *Vanir! Vanir!* Their leader, Angerboda, giggled meanly. "Sorry. We're allergic."

"To politeness?" quipped Skade. Since Skade was a half-giant, Angerboda didn't target her for teasing most of the time. So Skade could risk making a snarky comment back. But Angerboda was always picking on the other girls, especially Freya.

"Ha-ha, so funny I forgot to laugh," Freya said to the girlgiants. Thing was, somehow Angerboda had gotten the idea that Freya was crushing on Loki. (Which was *not* true.) Angerboda was so weird that she actually had a crush on that troublemaking boygod herself! The fact that he was a half-giant too might have had something to do with her feelings toward him.

Plop! Idun pushed back from the table as an ammo-herring fell short of its target and dropped into her soup instead, splattering her. "Ymir's nose!" she exclaimed.

The girlgiants glared at her. "What did you say?" Angerboda demanded.

Idun just rolled her eyes. *Argh!* Unfortunately, many giants had never gotten over having Ymir (one of their own kind) used by the gods of Asgard as some sort of giant seed from which to grow the nine worlds. Their annoyance was kind of understandable. Unfortunately, it caused them to make trouble for Asgard.

"Hey! Watch out for that . . . oops." Before Idun could finish issuing a warning, a wedge of frieze cheese smacked Angerboda on the forehead.

As her name suggested, *Anger*boda was quick to get angry over just about everything. Instantly she and her buds all shape-shifted into their ginormous giant-size selves.

"Who did that?" Angerboda demanded to know. Her head nearly touched the ceiling now as she glared around the room. When the offending warrior froze in fright, the girlgiants bounded off toward his frieze. Luckily this caused the food fight to shift away from Idun's and her friends' table for a while. Unluckily for Idun, however, it caused Freya's attention to focus on *her*.

"So I heard Loki teasing you after we all landed in the snow. What was that about?" Freya asked suddenly.

"Huh?" Idun blinked at the change in topic. Sure, she remembered how Loki had suggested that she was the apple of Bragi's eye. Meaning that Bragi was crushing on her. It had been a crazy thing to say, of course. And Loki had even admitted he'd been joking. But then, why had Bragi blushed and suddenly become tongue-tied?

Without thinking, Idun slid her dark brown eyes to

the table where Bragi and Loki sat with Thor and some other boygods. At the exact same moment she glanced Bragi's way, *his* eyes landed on *her*. They both looked away—fast.

Too late. Idun realized from her friends' raised eyebrows that they had seen her and Bragi's accidental eyelock. Freya sent her a knowing look as she opened her mouth, probably to ask what that was all about. She was the girlgoddess of love and beauty and sometimes acted like a romance detective!

Not wanting to talk about Bragi's maybe-or-maybe-not crush on her (not yet, anyway), Idun shrugged casually. "You know Loki. He's always teasing." Quickly she steered the conversation in another direction. "That make-believe troll incident was typical him, right?"

Sif took the bait. "Isn't *that* the truth. Wish there were some way we could take a vacation from his constant teasing."

"We did get a vacation," Skade reminded her.

"Remember? When his lips got sealed for a whole day?"

That had happened not long ago when that wily boygod had lost a bet to an angry dwarf. The prize had been Loki's head! Lucky for Loki, the dwarf had eventually settled for temporarily zipping Loki's lips.

Freya sighed happily at the memory. "Yeah, good times. Too bad we don't have the power to stop his tricks and troublemaking like that whenever we want."

"Hey, I know!" Skade exclaimed with a mischievous grin. "What if every time Loki tries one of his mean tricks, we bury him in the earth for a while, sort of like what happened to Ymir?"

"Or cut off his hair," Sif said with relish. "Although I guess that wouldn't be much of a punishment for him since his hair isn't magical, and he could just grow it back. Unlike me." She was the girlgoddess of bountiful harvests, and her hair's magic protected the golden fields of wheat that humans grew down in Midgard. When Loki had snipped off her hair (yet another one

67

of his awful tricks), Midgard's wheat had wilted and almost died!

"Good thing he got those dwarfs to spin you some *new* hair," Freya commented as Sif dug into her food. "Otherwise we'd be eating sandwiches without the bread. Which wouldn't really count as sandwiches!"

Her mouth full now, Sif only smiled and nodded in reply.

"Could you talk your tabby cats into scratching him anytime he tricks someone?" Skade suggested to Freya.

Her friends' talk of revenge was beginning to make Idun feel uncomfortable, no matter how much Loki deserved it. "Hello? Am I the only one at this table who remembers the whole reason Odin created this academy?" she said at last. "Wasn't it for us to learn to get along? To set a good example for all those who dwell in the nine worlds?"

"Yes, but that's not going to work unless a certain

yellow-shoe-wearing boygod meets us halfway," said Skade.

"Certain girlgiants, too," added Freya, her eyes flicking to Angerboda.

Suddenly those girlgiants exited the Valhallateria, and Idun and her friends found themselves in the middle of the food fight again. As they were bombarded by overripe, juicy cherries, Freya snatched up her bag. "Yikes, let's get out of here before our clothes are completely ruined!"

Leaving their almost-empty plates on the table for the Valkyrie cleanup crew, the girls jumped from their chairs and headed for the dining hall door. While they were fleeing the building, Idun thought about what her friends had said. They weren't always this grumpy and interested in getting even with Loki, but his troll stunt earlier had reminded them of all his other, even *worse*, stunts.

Thing was, a lot hung in the balance if Odin's social

experiment didn't succeed. If the academy's students weren't able to prove that they could get along, more wars would probably break out. Like the one between the Aesir and the Vanir that had led Odin to establish the academy in the first place. And that might hasten Ragnarok, a horrific doomsday event involving fire, fighting, and famine. That event would lead to the end of the nine worlds!

If she was right and there really was some goodness in Loki's heart, maybe she could help him become a better person somehow, Idun thought as she and her friends came to a stop outside the V. She recalled all the lectures Odin had given in the weeks since the academy opened—lectures encouraging students to form new friendships outside their usual groups. Maybe she should try to befriend Loki. Odin would surely want her to! But was it really possible to guide Loki toward better behavior?

Again, that Glad Rags sweater's prophecy came to

mind: "Do a good deed, and you'll get what you need."
Hmm. She eyed Freya's bag. In her humble opinion, what she *really* needed was that cloak! If she could come up with a good deed that would somehow get Loki to stop making trouble, maybe everyone, her included, would get what they needed.

"Worth a shot," she murmured under her breath.

4

Into the Forest

"NOT SO FAST!" A VOICE CALLED TO IDUN, Freya, Sif, and Skade outside the Valhallateria. It was Loki. Apparently he and Bragi had followed them out the door. "You weren't going to sneak off without showing me your shape-shifting cloak, were you?" Loki demanded of Freya.

"'Course not," Freya shot back. "Unlike you, when I make a promise, I don't try to trick my way out of it!"

Grinning at Loki, Bragi said, "I've no wish to offend, but she got you, my friend."

Loki scowled at him. "People claim you're a poet, but *I'd* never know it!"

"Good one!" Bragi declared, slapping him on the back good-naturedly. "Maybe being around me will turn you into a poet too, one of these days."

"No chance, poet pants!" Loki exclaimed. Then, realizing he'd rhymed by accident again, he sputtered, "I'd rather fight the flames of Ragnarok than spout goofy rhymes!"

He turned toward Freya. "C'mon. Let's go find a clearing." With that, he, Freya, and the others set off together down a fern-lined snowy path. It wandered through a forest of trees that grew under Yggdrasil's sheltering branches.

When Idun found herself walking next to Bragi, she seized the opportunity to question him. She was hoping to learn something about Loki that would inspire a good deed she could do to keep him out of trouble. "You know Loki pretty well, right?" she said to the curly haired boy.

"Sure," said Bragi. "We've been friends since pre-school. Plus, we're in the same dorm room here at AA."

Idun nodded. "So then maybe you know why he is the way he is? Always tricking and teasing?"

"Interesting question." Bragi's forehead wrinkled in thought. "Loki has always rubbed people the wrong way. Even when we were little kids," he said after a moment. "Once someone gets a certain reputation, it can be hard to lose it, right? So maybe Loki just keeps on acting rotten because he knows that's what everyone expects." He paused briefly before adding, "I know he can be hard to like sometimes. Probably the reason we're still friends is because I see something in him that others don't."

"What's that?" Idun asked, really curious to know.

Before Bragi could reply, they came even with the academy's Heartwood Library, located in the very heart of Yggdrasil's enormous trunk. From inside the trunk, Gullveig, the librarian's assistant (also formerly Freya's nanny in Vanaheim), waved to the group through an open window. "Hellooo, everyone! Sif, Mimir got those books about wheat farming that you asked for," she called out.

"Thanks!" Sif called back. "Can I come get them later? I'm kind of busy right now."

"One must never be too busy for books!" rumbled another voice from inside Yggdrasil's trunk. It was Mimir, the head librarian. Through the window Idun caught a glimpse of him beyond Gullveig. He was bobbing up and down atop his water slide. Mimir had become detached from his body sometime in the past. But he—or rather, his *head*—had been magically brought back to life by Odin. And now that's all he was—a head. One with lots of knowledge inside, which made him a perfect librarian.

"Okay," Sif replied. She peeled off from the group,

saying, "I'll catch up later. And I'll want details of how the flight went if I miss out. Good luck, Freya!" Returning Sif's farewell wave, Idun watched her go toward the library. Gullveig and Mimir were so helpful, Idun thought as she and Bragi followed Skade, Freya, and Loki through the forest. Helping others seemed to make them feel as happy as it made her feel.

Suddenly an idea popped into her head. What if her good deed could be to get Loki to do something to help others too? Which could improve his reputation. And maybe that would make him feel good about himself as well. Which might make him less likely to behave rottenly to everyone.

Before Idun could mull this idea over more, Bragi spoke again, pulling her attention. "You really want to know what I see in Loki that no one else sees?" he asked.

"Uh-huh," she replied as they walked along. Darting a look ahead, she saw that Skade, Freya, and Loki were

76

busily chatting. Good. Loki wouldn't hear whatever she and Bragi said about him.

"Here's the thing about Loki. He's smart and funny and fun to hang out with. And he *can* be nice, unless he's showing off. Even though he acts selfish—*mean*, too, occasionally—deep, deep, *deep* down I think he wants to be a good guy. He just acts without thinking sometimes. It's like he doesn't stop to consider the consequences."

"Really? That's what I sort of guessed," Idun exclaimed excitedly. She was glad she and Bragi thought alike on the topic of Loki.

Bragi nodded. "Remember how proud he was of himself after he got the dwarfs to make those gifts a while back?" The gifts had included Sif's replacement hair, Thor's hammer, and a cunning ship made of many small parts that fit together like a puzzle. The ship, whose name was *Skidbladnir*, could grow big enough to hold an entire army when unfolded and set in the sea!

Becoming uncharacteristically quiet, Bragi looked

down at his boots and kicked at the snowy ground. Finally, he spoke again. "Loki says a lot of things that aren't true. But some things he says are truer than he realizes."

Huh? Idun stared at him in confusion. She opened her mouth to ask what he meant, but then she recalled again how Loki had teased Bragi with his "apple of your eye" remark. Her face grew warm. Was Bragi hinting that Loki's comment about him being interested in her was truer than Loki realized?

As far as she knew, no boy had ever crushed on her before. The idea that Bragi might *like*-like her sent a jumble of emotions surging through her—shyness and panic, but also a little thrill of excitement. Unsure what to say in response, she desperately tried to think of a change of topic. Luckily, just then they arrived at the clearing Freya had been heading for, an area that served as a hub of sorts for travel to and from classes.

"Oh good, we're here," Idun said to Bragi. *Saved!*

All around the clearing, doors sort of like the golden ones Heimdall had sent them through earlier hovered in midair at various heights with no visible means of support. These were magical portals used to transport students to their Asgard Academy classrooms.

Eyeing her and Bragi, Loki said impatiently, "Took you guys long enough!" He was leaning against a sign that indicated which of the hovering doors led to which class halls. It had always delighted Idun that not all the doors were boring rectangles. Some were shaped like circles or triangles or trapezoids, or even objects and animals.

Besides the various doors, numerous small rainbow bridges could be seen among the trees that bordered the clearing. The doors and bridges, as well as a series of branch ladders, vine tunnels, vine swings, and vine slides, allowed students to travel up, down, and around Yggdrasil's branches to get from place to place. Since it was Sunday, there were no classes, but there were other students hanging out in the clearing, including a few girls playing Spydkast.

Asgard Academy was way more beautiful and interesting than the school Idun had gone to before coming here. She liked AA's classes, the other kids, and the whole magical feeling of the academy much better than her old school. It was another reason she hoped Odin's getting-along experiment would succeed. Because if AA failed, they'd all have to return home!

Now that Bragi and Idun had arrived, Loki glanced over at Freya and yelled, "Let's get this shape-shifting show on the road!"

Freya rolled her eyes. "Hang on, Mr. Impatient!" she scolded Loki. She and Skade had been chatting together, probably about the upcoming flight. However, now Freya did what Loki asked and withdrew her falcon feather cloak from her bag.

"Fly away with me!" the cloak said at once.

The boys' eyes bugged out when they saw and heard

the cloak. "I don't mean to gawk, but did that thing just talk?" Bragi asked.

"Mm-hmm," Freya said.

"Who cares if it's a chatterbox," Loki said with a frown. "I want to see what else it can do!"

Freya glanced at Idun and Skade. From the look on her face, Idun guessed that she was feeling reluctant about going on with the demonstration. But Freya had promised that Loki could see her cloak in action. Idun knew that she wouldn't go back on that promise.

Noting Freya's hesitation, Skade said, "Might as well show them. They'll find out sooner or later."

Nodding, Freya shrugged off her red wool cloak at last. She handed it and her empty bag to Skade. Then she draped the feathered cloak over her shoulders. As before, it tightened around her instantly, clinging to her like a feathered skin. *Whoosh!* Two wings opened grandly from its sides. Freya's legs and feet became claws. Her head transformed into that of a sharp-beaked falcon.

81

With a high-pitched cry, she rose into the sky above the clearing and began to circle overhead.

The boys' jaws dropped. Idun could see that they were impressed. "Whoa! Wow!" they exclaimed. Others in the clearing saw Freya rise too. They pointed, shouting and clapping.

That could've been me, thought Idun. If only she were the one wowing them instead! She squashed down the jealous feeling and tried to feel happy for Freya.

Chuk, chuk! Just then, a big nosy squirrel named Ratatosk appeared on the limb of one of the trees at the edge of the clearing. A knapsack of message acorns was slung over his back. His adorable little acorns, with their cute faces and hats and babyish voices, were a little nutty. But they were also fun and helpful. They delivered news all over the nine worlds, wherever Ratatosk dropped them off.

Noticing that everyone was looking up, the squirrel hopped over to the branch of a tree closer to the action for a better view. As he watched falcon-Freya wheeling around in the sky, he rubbed his front paws together and eagerly called out to the students. "That's some big bird! What's going on?"

"Just watching it fly," Skade said.

"Yeah, nothing's going on. See you later," hinted Idun. She was hoping the squirrel would leave. Sharing too much information with Ratatosk was never a good idea. Besides delivering message acorns, this busybody squirrel ran up and down between the worlds spreading *gossip*. Usually messed-up, scrambled gossip.

Whoosh! Unfortunately, falcon-Freya chose the very next moment to land near Loki. Shrugging off her cloak, she returned to her goddess form.

"Aha!" Ratatosk exclaimed, twitching his tail in delight. "I knew that bird was no ordinary falcon!" The squirrel scampered from the tree with his knapsack of acorn messengers. Lickety-split, he scooted down the path, leaving paw prints in the snow.

"Uh-oh. Looks like your cloak secret is officially out," Idun informed Freya, watching him go.

Skade nodded. "By tomorrow all nine worlds will have heard about it."

"Who cares?" said Freya. Flying and impressing these boys seemed to have put her in a good mood. She arched an eyebrow at Loki as she folded her feather cloak over one arm. "Well?" she said with a grin. "What do you think of my shape-shifting cloak?"

"It's awesome," Bragi blurted out before Loki could reply.

Loki scowled at him. Then, looking at Freya, he shrugged. "It's okay."

Freya sniffed. "Just *okay*?"

"It works, obviously," Loki said. "But . . . well . . ." He hesitated a moment, then silently shook his head. "Never mind. It's not important."

Freya jutted out her chin. "What's not important? Say it!"

Loki gestured toward the cloak distastefully. "Fine. Aren't feather clothes kind of weird? I mean, I don't see other girls wearing feathers."

Freya's face slowly crumpled. As the girlgoddess of love and beauty, her appearance was very important to her. "M-maybe you're right," she said uncertainly. "Maybe feathers aren't my style. What was I thinking?"

She stared at the cloak as if it were an old dishrag. Suddenly seeming strangely eager to be rid of it, she said brightly, "Want it, Loki? Because I don't." She held it out to him.

Idun, Bragi, and Skade all stared at her, shocked that she would offer Loki her cloak even if it wasn't her style.

I'll take it! Idun almost shouted out. But she stopped herself when she noticed a twinkle in Freya's eye. That girlgoddess was up to something.

Loki shrugged. Casually he said, "It's not really my style either. But I suppose I could take it off your hands." He reached for the cloak. However, before he could touch a single feather, Freya snatched it back, pressing it to her chest.

"Ha!" she exclaimed. "You're not nearly as clever as you think, Loki. Did you really believe you could trick me out of this amazing cloak by making me doubt how I look?"

Playfully Bragi thumped Loki on the back. "Freya's quick. She guessed your trick!"

To his credit, Loki shook off any embarrassment and grinned. "Can't blame me for trying." To Freya he said, "It's cool. You're lucky you found it.

"Gotta go," he told everyone. "I'm meeting up with Honir at the dorm to go hiking down in Midgard. He wants to show me some mountain that he likes to climb in Thrymheim along the border between Midgard and Jotunheim." He turned toward Bragi. "Want to come?"

"Sure," Bragi told him. As Loki started trotting in the direction of the dorms, Bragi jogged after him a ways and then turned back to the girls to wave. "See ya!" He shot Idun a smile and blushed again.

"Wouldn't wanna be ya!" Loki added to the girls, rhyming with a laugh.

"Hope they take a map," Freya said to Idun and Skade after the boys took off. "I wouldn't trust Honir to know his way around an *ant*hill. He's kind of clueless." Quickly she donned her red wool cloak again.

"Yeah, I know he rooms with them and all, but I wouldn't follow him anywhere," Skade agreed. Taking Freya's feather cloak from her, she stuffed it back in its bag.

With that, the three of them headed for Vingolf Hall, the girls' dorm. "Honir's got superlong legs, so I bet he's a good hiker, though," Idun said. Maybe he wasn't the brightest guy, but Freya and Skade were being kind of mean about him.

"I hope so. Jotunheim is giant territory—not the safest place to go hiking. Not all giants are as nice as I am," Skade noted matter-of-factly.

"Still, they do seem to be in awe of that mighty

hammer Thor got. Ever since he started patrolling the wall around Asgard, they haven't been coming around causing trouble like they used to," said Idun.

Up ahead, she watched Bragi and Loki catch hold of the vine swing that would take them to a round door that went directly to Breidablik Hall, the boys' dorm. Just before they were lifted away, Idun saw Loki glance over his shoulder at the bag containing Freya's cloak. There was a certain glint in his eyes, full of emotion. Having felt that emotion herself, she was pretty sure she recognized what it was.

Jealousy.

5
The Golden Apples

"I THINK BRAGI LIKES YOU," FREYA ANNOUNCED

to Idun as they and Skade headed for vine swings too.

"You d-do?" Idun sputtered. She felt a flush spread over her cheeks.

"What?" said Skade, sounding surprised. She cocked her head at Idun, studying her speculatively. "So Bragi's crushing on you?"

"No way! I barely even know him," Idun protested, even though she'd been wondering the very same thing.

Although she and Bragi hadn't spoken to each other much before today, it did seem like they were starting to be friends. But more than just friends? *No,* she decided firmly. That was a silly idea.

Just then Sif came along, carrying her library books. "So? How was the flight?"

"Fantastic!" said Freya.

"Yeah! Wait till you hear," said Skade. "Loki and Bragi were super impressed. Tell her, Freya."

Deciding this was a good time to make a getaway, Idun snapped her fingers as if a thought had just come to her. "Hey! Just remembered I'm late for picking my apples to take to the V kitchen. See you all later back at Vingolf!" she called to her friends. Then she scurried over to a nearby branch ladder. Normally, she picked her apples in the early mornings so they'd be fresh and available for meals all day. So what she'd said was true. But she also wanted to avoid further questions about crushes!

With a farewell wave to Sif and the others, Idun

90

climbed down the branch ladder. Once she reached the bottom, she disappeared into a familiar vine tunnel. One that led to the small grove of golden apples that were hers alone to tend.

There was a total of nine trees in the pretty grove, same as the number of worlds protected beneath Yggdrasil's branches. She walked among the trees, relaxed by the whispering sound their leaves made in greeting. She lifted her fingers to brush against those leaves, her way of greeting them back.

Every day, each of these trees produced nine perfect, magical golden apples. Eighty-one apples in all. Plucking them from the trees was a task that only she could do. Because if anyone else—even Odin himself—were to so much as just touch one of the apples while it still clung to a tree, the apple would shrivel and disappear in a puff of smoke. *Poof!* However, when Idun picked an apple, it would remain firm and juicy and sweet for days or even years—until it was eaten.

Stopping to stand at the center of her apple grove, Idun pulled a tiny wooden box called an *eski* from the pocket of her *hangerock*. When she gave her *eski* a shake and set it on the ground, it quickly expanded from the size of a single ice cube into a box large enough to hold today's crop of apples. This magical wooden box made of ash wood went with her everywhere. Though it was now as tall as her knees and wide enough that she could've sat inside it, it could be folded to pocket-size again (much like the ship *Skidbladnir*) when not in use.

"Okay, time to get to work," Idun murmured to her trees. She reached up for an apple, gave it a twist, and pulled at an angle. This was the proper way to pluck an apple. *Snap!* It broke free of the tree. She set the apple gently into her *eski*. Some of the apples grew so high that they were out of reach. No problem. As she approached each tree, its branches gracefully bent lower to allow her to pick its apples without need of a ladder.

Tug, twist, toss. Tug, twist, toss. In no time the *eski* was full. As always, Idun thanked her trees for their apples and uttered a chant that would keep the trees healthy, strong, and productive even during the long Nordic winters.

> *"Despite cold and snow,*
> *May you prosper and grow.*
> *Despite ice and sleet,*
> *May your apples be sweet."*

Ready to leave now, she gave her apple-heavy *eski* a tap. Instantly sled runners dropped from the bottom of it so it could easily glide over snow and ice. When she bent to push the *eski* from behind, the trees sighed and swayed, waving goodbye. Idun waved back. Then she was off to deliver the apples to the V kitchen staff.

She was halfway to the Valhallateria when her apples gave her an idea. An idea for a good deed she and Loki could do together. If she could get him to agree, he would be helping others. And, fingers crossed, his helpful act would improve his reputation and also make *him* feel good!

Excited about her idea, Idun pushed her *eski* faster and faster over the snowy ground. She couldn't wait to suggest it to Loki. But then she remembered that he had gone hiking with Bragi and Honir. Drat. All fired up about her good deed idea, she wished she could share it with Loki right now. But it would keep.

When she came upon a downward sloping hill, she stepped to stand on the back end of the *eski*'s runners. The cold air made her gasp as the *eski* whipped down the slope, with her perched behind it. Wondering how the boys' mountain trek was going, she zoomed toward the V with her apples. *Whee!*

6
The Regal Eagle

BRAGI STARED UP AT THE FEW SNOWFLAKES that were drifting lazily down from the mostly clear sky. While Idun was delivering her precious apples of youth to the Valhallateria kitchen, he'd gone hiking with Honir and Loki. Well, hiking and *skiing*. Hiking on the bare patches of ground here and there and then skiing in places where the snow became too thick for walking.

"Hurry up, slowpokes!" Honir called out. Standing

halfway up a snowcapped craggy mountainside, he waited for Loki and Bragi to catch up.

After taking the Bifrost Bridge to Midgard, the three boygods had put on their cross-country skis before crossing a snowy valley to the mountainside they were now climbing. Unlike the downhill kind, these skis attached to their boots at the toe, not the heel. This allowed them to use more of a skating motion while moving across flat ground and up and down short slopes.

"It's slow going in these steep mountains," said Loki, huffing and puffing his way up the trail they were following.

"Not if you have long legs like me," Honir said with a chuckle.

"The views from up here are phenomenal," Bragi enthused, gazing down at the Midgard farms and villages below.

There had been brief snow showers as the boys went along, but then the skies would turn clear, like now. "The more we travel higher, the more I wish I'd brought my lyre," Bragi rhymed. Creating lyrics was always easier when he strummed it.

"Yeah, I wish you had it too. I could use it for a sled," said Loki. It was kind of a lame joke, but Bragi cracked up anyway. Loki really could be funny.

After the boys caught up to Honir, he pushed off again. Bragi kept a short distance behind Loki as they all zigzagged their way farther up the mountain. The long-legged Honir was soon ahead of them again by at least thirty strides and widening the distance. He was a little (Okay, a lot!) forgetful and didn't have the sharpest mind, but he was probably one of the top skiers at the academy.

"Honir, wait up!" Bragi shouted.

"'Kay!" Honir stopped in the middle of the trail to let them catch up once more.

"Ymir's knees! I'm starving!" Loki said as soon as he and Bragi drew even with Honir again.

97

"Me too," said Bragi. He pointed to Honir's backpack. "Why don't you break out the snacks you brought?"

"Snacks?" Honir echoed blankly.

Loki frowned at him. "You volunteered to get food from the V before we left. Don't tell me you forgot!"

"No, I didn't forget," Honir said defensively. But there was a look of worry and confusion in his brown eyes.

"Here, let me check your backpack," Bragi told him.

"Sure. Okay," Honir said agreeably, smiling again.

Bragi stepped his skis sideways until he stood directly behind Honir. After he undid the pack's straps and lifted the top flap to look inside, his stomach sank. "Empty," he reported to Loki.

"Like Honir's head! And my stomach!" Loki frowned at the long-legged boygod. "This is great, just great," he said sarcastically. "So you *did* forget to bring snacks."

"Or maybe you forgot you were supposed to share them and ate everything already?" Bragi asked.

Honir scrunched up his eyebrows and tapped his chin with a gloved finger as if thinking hard. "No," he said at last. "I'm hungry too, so I can't have eaten any snacks." Then his eyes lit up. "I remember now! I went to the V to get snacks, but there were too many things to choose from, like apple turnovers, bread, cheese, porridge, and hard-boiled eggs. I couldn't decide." He paused. "I went to ask you guys what to choose, but then when I saw you, you were ready to go. So I went with you." He smiled at them. "And here we are."

"Yeah, without snacks. Thanks a lot," Loki said, rolling his eyes.

Honir just shrugged good-naturedly. "Sorry."

His reply seemed to anger Loki even more. "Yeah, well, you should be, loser!"

"Insults aren't going to help," Bragi said quickly. When Loki got hungry (and he was almost always hungry), he could get hangry. Hungry plus angry, that is. Bragi looked back the way they'd come. "If we turn around now, we can probably reach Asgard in two hours. Maybe even sooner since it's mostly downhill."

Honir pointed to the top of the mountain they were on. "Or if we keep going, we could eat at the café up there," he suggested. "It's only maybe a half hour away."

"Café?" Bragi and Loki echoed at the same time.

"You mean there's a restaurant at the top?" Bragi asked. He squinted, but the cloud cover was so thick higher up that he couldn't see if there was a building there or not.

"Yeah." Honir nodded. "It's called the Regal Eagle Café."

"Catchy name," said Bragi.

Honir grinned and elbowed him. "You like anything that rhymes."

"Okay. Let's go!" Loki grunted. "Before I waste away to bones." He skied off fast and the other two followed, continuing their upward trek. Sure enough, when some clouds shifted a few minutes later, they caught sight of a building with a steeply pitched, snow-covered roof at the top of the mountain.

A half hour later, completely famished by now, the three boys stood outside the small wooden-sided café. They quickly slipped off their skis and stood them near the door, then clomped into the café in their boots. As they stepped inside, a delicious smell greeted them.

"Mm-mm," said Loki. Inhaling deeply, he smiled in delight. "Now that's what I'm talking about!" Since there were no other customers in the café, they took seats at the nearest of the four empty tables.

Across the room, a six-foot-tall eagle wearing a gold crown stood with its back to them. It had a huge soup ladle clutched in one claw and was using it to stir a gigantic pot of soup over a large firepit. Smoke from the fire drifted upward to escape through a large hole at the top of the ceiling.

"The owner," Honir whispered.

"Explains the café's name," Bragi murmured.

"Hello?" Loki yelled toward the eagle.

"*Scree-ee! Scree-ee!*" it exclaimed, ruffling its feathers in surprise. It hadn't noticed them until Loki had called out. Now the large eagle bustled over to the boys' table. "Theaks reakt. Neak wheak'll eak beak?" it said. (At least that's what it sounded like to Bragi.)

"Huh?" all three boys responded at once.

"Oh, sorry. You're boygods, right?" said the eagle. "Of course you wouldn't understand eaglespeak."

"Beakspeak?" Loki echoed, mangling the word. On purpose, no doubt, Bragi guessed.

The eagle clicked his hooked yellow beak, making a tsk sound. Bragi eyed the beak nervously, thinking it looked rather lethal. "*Eagle*speak. My language," corrected the eagle. "Anyway, welcome to the Regal Eagle. What can I get you, beaks? I mean, boys?"

"What've you got?" Loki asked, rubbing his hands together in anticipation.

The eagle cocked his head toward the firepit. "How about some tasty oxtail soup?"

"And what else?" Loki asked expectantly. "We worked up huge appetites skiing up this mountain."

The eagle shrugged and then used its beak to preen the feathers at its neck. "Oxtail soup. That's it. The whole menu."

"That's why I love this place," Honir told the other two boys. "No decisions to make about what to order."

"Fine," huffed Loki. "I'm going to need a gallon of that soup, though. Maybe two gallons."

The eagle nodded. "Sure. There's just one thing, though. Whatever you order, I get to eat my fill of it first before I serve you. House rule."

Honir scrunched up his eyebrows like he was thinking hard again. "Yup," he said at last. "I remember that from the last time I was here."

"Okay, whatever," Loki said reluctantly.

"Yeah, whatever! We'll be happy if service is snappy!" Bragi rhymed.

"Right, then." The eagle hopped back to the firepit. It grabbed the edge of the soup pot with both claws, lifted it high, and tipped the top edge of it down toward its open beak. Then it proceeded to guzzle down the soup in huge gulps. *Glug, glug, glug.*

Guessing that the eagle meant to finish all the soup in the pot, Loki jumped up from the table. "Stop!" he yelled. But the eagle just fixed him with a beady eye and kept on gulping. As the eagle tipped the pot, the ladle fell from it. Grabbing it up, Loki swung it at the big bird like a sword. "Drop that pot, eagle! Or else!"

"Happy to oblige," said the eagle, who had finished the soup by now, and so dropped the pot. With one clawed foot, he grabbed the bowl end of the ladle as Loki swung it at him again. As Loki held fast to the handle end, the eagle chanted some sort of magic spell that went like this: "Deaked leaked geak!"

Letting out a high-pitched screech, the eagle flapped its wings. *Whoosh!* Still grasping the bowl of the ladle, the eagle soared up toward the smoke hole in the ceiling above the firepit.

Not letting go of *his* end, Loki got dragged up there too! "Help!" he shouted down as they neared the hole.

Bragi and Honir began to laugh. It was a hilarious sight.

"Help!" Loki shrieked again.

Feeling sorry for him, Bragi yelled, "Just let go of the handle!"

"Don't you think I would if I could?" Loki called out. "My hands are stuck to it! Some kind of magic at work!"

After Loki disappeared through the smoke hole, Bragi and Honir ran outside. They scooped up rocks from the ground and threw them at the eagle, trying to make it let loose of Loki. Unfortunately, half of Honir's rocks went straight up. As they plummeted back down again, he and Bragi had to leap aside to avoid being hit. In the end, their efforts didn't matter. Already, the kooky cook bird had flown Loki too high and too far away.

The eagle laughed. *Scree-ee! Scree-ee!* It dipped lower as it started down the mountainside, causing Loki's feet to drag on the ground and bang against boulders and trees.

"Ow! Ow! Let me go!" the boys heard Loki cry out. But the regal eagle pretended not to hear.

"We can't just stand around and listen to him yelp," said Honir.

"Then let's ski down and try to help!" Bragi replied.

Quickly the two boys strapped on their skis. "So you've been to the Regal Eagle Café before, right?" Bragi asked Honir as they took off. They each balanced one of Loki's skis over a shoulder as they zoomed down the mountainside, swerving around trees and boulders.

"Yup," Honir replied as they gained speed. "Twice."

"Did you actually get to eat anything either time?" Bragi asked, totally puzzled.

"Nope," Honir called back as they hit a straight stretch and he pulled ahead. "Forgot about that part till now."

Bragi's stomach was rumbling with hunger, but Honir was Honir. No use getting mad at him for just being *him*. They'd simply have to wait to eat till they were back at the academy. First, they had to rescue Loki. But how?

Much to Bragi's surprise, as he was pondering various schemes, the eagle suddenly released Loki. *Oomph!* Loki fell flat on his back in the powdery snow.

"Whoa!" yelled Bragi and Honir. They swerved to avoid running him over. Once beyond their hapless roommate, they turned the front tips of their skis inward and snowplowed to a stop. Then they skied back to the fallen boygod.

"You okay?" Bragi asked.

Loki sat up with a groan. "Yeah, just bruised and a little pecked." Pointing in the direction the big bird had flown, he added, "That was no eagle. It was a giant in disguise. Told me his name was Thiazi."

"How did you finally overcome his magic to get free of that soup ladle handle?" Bragi asked.

"I . . . uh . . . I dunno . . . I just did," Loki said evasively. He leaped up and grabbed his skis from the other boys. "Thanks for bringing these." Changing the subject, he added, "Let's get back to Asgard. I'm so hungry I could eat my boots!"

"Ditto," said Bragi.

"Me three," said Honir.

Without further discussion, the very hungry boys skied off. Looking over his shoulder, Bragi noticed that the pesky eagle had flown down to perch atop the café roof. His beak was curved in an evil, knowing smile. Bragi wondered about that smile the rest of the way down the mountainside, across the valley, and as they hiked up the Bifrost Bridge to Asgard. Could there be something Loki wasn't telling them?

7

V Chat

IDUN HAD JUST TAKEN A GULP OF APPLE JUICE when the Valhallateria's double doors burst open. *Boom!* Startled, she looked over to see Bragi, Honir, and Loki rush into the cafeteria like they were starving. Their hair was tangled, their cheeks cherry red from the cold and wind.

Only moments ago she'd plonked down at this table, sitting across from Yanis, a light-elf girl with sunny yellow hair, and Malfrid, a red-haired human girl. She hadn't sat with them this year so far. Both girls were nice, if a little giggly. By joining their table, Idun was following the rule about having at least one daily meal with others she didn't usually sit with.

Her roomies were doing the same. Skade was sitting with some of her frosty girlgiant friends from Jotunheim and two light-elf boys. Freya, with her brother, Frey, and boys named Njord and Kvasir (all Vanir) plus a couple of Aesir kids. Since the Vanir and Aesir had been enemies during the war, that was pretty cool. And Sif was seated with some dwarfs from the world of Darkalfheim.

"I know we're supposed to forge friendships among the different worlds," Yanis said now, pulling Idun's attention. "But I'm glad no fire giants go to school here. I'd be afraid to befriend them."

"Don't worry. I heard they aren't allowed out of Muspelheim," said Malfrid.

"Good thing," Idun commented. "Their abilities

with fire might come in handy with cooking in the V kitchen, though."

"Or maybe not, since those fire giants burn whatever they touch!" said Yanis, her eyes wide.

Idun nodded. "True." No one she knew had ever seen a fire giant, but they'd all heard horrible stories about them.

"Hey, nothing wrong with a little fire," said a voice. The girls looked up to see Loki standing near their table. "Mind if I sit with you?" he asked, surprising all three girls. Without waiting for a reply, he plopped into the empty chair on Idun's right. Immediately he grabbed a bread roll from a basket that sat at the center of the table and gobbled it down. "I'm the boygod of fire, remember?" he said, while reaching for a second roll. "Unrelated to fire giants, of course."

Although this wasn't actually funny, Yanis and Malfrid giggled.

"Okay if I sit with you guys too?" Bragi asked Idun.

He gestured to the chair on her other side. He'd followed Loki over while Honir had gone to sit elsewhere.

"Nope. Sorry. You know Odin's rule," Loki told him. He'd gobbled down his second roll even faster than the first. "We're supposed to mingle, remember? You were at my same table at breakfast and lunch, so sit somewhere else." He flicked his fingers, indicating that Bragi should go, then grabbed a third roll since the Valkyries hadn't yet appeared with their food trays.

"Suddenly you're a rule-follower?" Bragi asked, laughing. But he smiled gamely at Idun and the other two girls. "Later," he told them all. Then he headed off to another table.

The minute he left, Yanis and Malfrid giggled again, sending glances Bragi's way. They were acting like they were crushing on him! Though she couldn't have said just why, Idun did not like the idea. *It's none of your beeswax if they like him,* she told herself.

She tuned them out and turned to Loki with a bright

smile. "I'm glad you're here because I actually want to talk to you." For a brief moment she wasn't sure he'd heard her. His eyes were glued to the Valkyries, who had just appeared from the kitchen and begun to fly about the room setting places and handing out steaming plates of roast pork, potatoes, peas, and apple fritters. "Hello?" She snapped her fingers to get his attention.

Loki turned her way as a Valkyrie appeared at their table. "Sorry, Idun. I heard you. And I want to talk to you too." He snagged a plate of food from the Valkyrie's tray before she could hand them around. She scowled but didn't scold him as she passed plates to the three girls.

"Oh? What about?" Idun asked digging in to her food. A little pang of dismay struck her when she noticed Yanis take a couple of bites of her apple fritter, then push it to the far side of her plate. Same with Malfrid. Their actions reminded her of her friends seeming disinterested in her apple chips this morning.

What was going on with everybody and her apples all of a sudden, anyway?

"You go first," Loki said to Idun, around a mouthful of pork and potato. "If I don't eat, I'll keel over. Honir forgot to bring snacks on our ski trip." With that, he stuffed his entire fritter into his mouth. At least *he* was eating her apples, but then he was pretty much gobbling everything in sight.

"Okay," said Idun, staring in amazement at the way he was shoveling food down. While his mouth was full, it gave her the perfect opportunity to tell him about the good deed she had in mind for them. She glanced over at Yanis and Malfrid to see if they were listening in. She didn't really want anyone else to hear about her idea. Not yet, anyway.

At that moment, the two girls spotted Bragi heading for Heidrun. They drank the contents of their *hrimkalders* fast, then jumped up and went to join him at the fountain for a refill.

Idun felt strangely annoyed as she watched them chatting with Bragi. Shaking her head to clear it, she chided herself for wasting time worrying over what those girls were up to. Now was her chance, while Loki's mouth was full and her tablemates were gone, to convince the boygod to help her carry out her good deed plan.

Quickly she said, "I was wondering . . . would you come with me to plant apple seeds down in Midgard? Like, maybe tomorrow morning?"

Loki gulped down another huge bite of roast pork. "I thought magic apples couldn't grow from seeds," he said in surprise.

"They can't. We'd be planting regular apple seeds," Idun explained. "Starting a new regular apple orchard to help out the humans in Midgard."

"Ha! Why would I want to help them?" Loki asked. Switching his empty plate for Yanis's full one, he began shoveling down her potatoes mixed with peas.

Knowing Loki, Idun had anticipated that he might ask such a question. So now she spoke the ready answer that she'd practiced in her head. "I don't know if you realize it," she said gently, so as not to hurt his feelings, "but you've got kind of a bad reputation here at the academy."

Loki's eyebrows rose at this. While his mouth was still full of food, making it hard for him to reply, Idun raced on. "Some people think you'll never change, but I don't believe that. I'm positive you have a good heart. And helping to plant seeds in Midgard will prove it. Besides," she enthused, "it feels great to do stuff for others. You'll see!"

She'd come to the end of her well-practiced little speech. Suddenly unsure of the effect it would have on Loki, she braced for a snarky reply. But none came.

Instead, in a sincere-sounding voice, he said, "Thanks, Idun. It's super nice of you to try to help me. Especially since no one else around here does. I can't say if you're right about me having a good heart, but okay, I'll give it a shot. I'll help plant seeds." Giving her his most winning smile, he reached over with his fork and nabbed the fritter from Malfrid's plate.

"You will?" Wow! Idun couldn't believe how easy it had been to convince him. Yay! She was kind of surprised and skeptical at his description of how others here at Asgard Academy treated him, though. Bragi was nice to him, at least.

Loki shrugged. "Yeah, why not? Long as we don't start too early. I need my beauty sleep," he joked. Having cleaned his and Yanis's plates, he now snagged a new one heaped with food off the large platter of a passing Valkyrie.

As he dug in to the new plate, Idun thoughtfully grabbed another full one for Yanis, too. "Okay, so when is a good time?" she asked eagerly. If she didn't pin Loki down now, she was afraid he might back out.

"I don't know. Around nine? We could meet at your

grove, so you could pick your apples before we leave."
He smiled at her.

"Sure." Idun smiled back, pleased. At least someone
around here still appreciated her apples!

"One thing," Loki said. "Don't tell anyone about this
seed planting plan, okay? I don't want people to think
I'm a good deed doer." He grinned. "Let people find out
on their own so it's not like I'm bragging."

"Oh, okay," Idun agreed. Before they could talk
more, Yanis and Malfrid returned to the table, their
refilled *hrimkalders* brimming with apple juice.

"What? You didn't bring any for me?" Loki teased
Yanis.

The elfgirl laughed a merry, bubbly laugh. "Just
a sec!" After setting down her *hrimkalder*, she skipped,
cartwheeled, and twirled her way back to Heidrun
to get a glass of juice for Loki. Light-elves were like
that—lighthearted.

Idun had to admire the boygod of fire sometimes.

Unlike her, when there was something Loki wanted, he had no trouble saying so. He didn't worry about appearing selfish. And more often than not this mischievous boy could get others to happily do what he wanted.

Since the girls were back now, was Bragi at his table too? Idun sneaked a peek. He was. Out of the corner of her eye she noticed him looking at her and Loki with a concerned—or maybe *unhappy*—look on his face. He wasn't close enough to have heard what they'd been talking about. So why the frown? Did he maybe thin that she and Loki were crushing on each other?

For some reason, she wished she could go over tell Bragi that they weren't. But what if she'd re wrong? He might just look at her like she was w say, *Who cares if you guys are crushing? Not me!*

Instead, she promised herself that as and Loki were back from Midgard tomorr Bragi and explain about her good deed Loki didn't want everyone to know ab

swear Bragi to secrecy.) Fingers crossed that she'd be able say that their seed planting had gone great.

Idun's eyes shifted to Freya's table as that girlgoddess rose to leave. Noticing the uneaten apple remains on everyone's plates, her throat tightened. Freya and her brother and friends had eaten barely enough apple to feel the effects of its youthful powers. *Do a good deed, and you'll get what you need.* What she needed right now was to know why no one was eating her apples!

When Freya, Sif, and Skade beckoned to her from the door a few seconds later, Idun quickly said goodbye to Loki, Yanis, and Malfrid. Leaving her empty plate on the table, she went to join her friends. She was planning to ask them her apple question on the way to Vingolf Hall, but before she got a chance, they all split off in different directions to go do different activities. It was only as she entered their dorm alone a few minutes later that she realized Loki had never told her what it was he'd wanted to talk to *her* about.

8
Loki Helps Out

IDUN WAS ALREADY PICKING HER GOLDEN apples of youth when Loki arrived in her cozy little nine-tree apple grove the next morning. Knowing it would be crisp and cold during the early morning hours, she'd worn her warmest wool stockings and snow boots. And she'd wrapped herself in her forest-green wool cloak, the hem of which she'd decorated with a border of embroidered apple blossoms. It was reversible, so she could also wear it with its red side out when she chose.

She stretched an arm up and a branch bowed low to meet her reaching hand. *Snap!* As the precious apple came away in her palm, the tree branch, lighter now without the apple's weight, bounced upward again, its leaves rustling.

She greeted Loki with a smile as she placed the apple she'd just picked alongside the others in her *eski*. "You're right on time."

Strung around her neck were two leather pouches. After lifting one free, she held it out to him. "Here," she said.

"What's this?" he asked, looking puzzled as he took it.

"Your half of the apple seeds," she explained. Then she tugged her favorite knit hat—the yellow one with the brown felt stem and green felt leaf—down to cover the tops of her cold ears. "I gather them whenever I'm out walking and come upon apple trees—non-magic ones, I mean," she explained further.

When Loki still appeared confused, she added,

"These are the seeds we'll be scattering down in Midgard today, remember?" Could he have forgotten *already*? Why did he think they were meeting here if not for that?

"Oh, yeah!" Loki exclaimed. "*Those* seeds. Sure, I remember. Just got a lot on my mind is all." Without bothering to look inside his pouch, he lowered its string over his head till the pouch hung around his neck. Then, eyeing the decorative painting she'd done on the front of her *eski*, he nodded appreciatively. "You're a good artist."

"Thanks," said Idun. Though pleased at the compliment, she knew that Loki rarely gave one unless he wanted something from someone. So when he gazed longingly at the golden apples in her half-full *eski*, she gestured toward them, saying, "Want one?"

He patted his stomach. "Yeah, but I'm full, so I'll wait till later. We're taking them all with us to Midgard, right?"

"Huh?" Idun said in surprise. "I thought we'd drop most of them at the V kitchen before we head out." She gave her *eski* a tap, causing its sled runners to drop from its flat bottom. "A stop there won't take too long."

Frowning, Loki grabbed onto her *eski* and wheeled it around to head for the bridge that would take them to Midgard. "But the kitchen's in the opposite direction. Let's just get going. I'll push."

"Well, we could just leave the *eski* here instead," she said, scurrying after him as he took off for the Bifrost Bridge. "No one will mess with it. I mean, we don't need to bring *all* of my apples."

"'Scuse me? You saw me wolfing down dinner last night, right? I have a humongous appetite." He nodded at the contents of her decorated cart. "If we didn't have to share with the rest of the boygods and girlgoddesses around here, I could probably devour all these scrumptious apples myself! Anyway, it'll be more fun with your *eski*. C'mon!" He began running with the cart, kicking his heels out behind him in an exaggerated way that was obviously meant to make her laugh.

And laugh she did. Letting Loki have his way, she ran along beside him and her cart until they were breathless. Truthfully, she felt flattered that he liked her apples so much. At least someone did.

Slowing somewhat, Loki gestured over his shoulder back toward her nine trees. Fruit still hung from some of them. "Want me to help you pick the rest of those apples later?" he asked.

"That's so nice of you!" said Idun. "But only I can do the picking. Anyone else touches an apple on those trees, and the apple withers."

Loki snapped his fingers. "Oh, yeah. I'd forgotten that," he said with a grin. Briefly Idun wondered if that was a lie and he'd only made his helpful offer because he knew she couldn't take him up on it. But today was about giving Loki the benefit of the doubt, so she did.

He grabbed an apple from her cart as they continued toward the bridge and then handed the cart off to her.

"So you aren't tired of my apples?" she asked, watching him munch the one he'd chosen.

"Why would I be?" he asked in surprise, looking over at her.

"It's just that I've been getting the funny feeling that some people around here are a little bored with them," she informed him.

"Yeah," Loki said. "I've noticed that too, actually. Maybe it's not the apples. Maybe it's the apple *recipes*. Why don't you shake things up? Have the kitchen try some new ones," he suggested.

Idun brightened. If that was all it was, she could fix that, easy! "Do you know any?" she asked eagerly. "Recipes, that is."

"Me? Nah, I don't know how to cook," said Loki. Finishing his apple, he tossed away the core. He didn't offer to take over pushing her *eski* again. But that was okay with Idun. It slid along easily on its runners. She wasn't really a cook either, but racking her brain as they walked along, she named off some recipe possibilities.

"Apple burgers?" she suggested.

Loki shook his head. "Frey doesn't like any food with the word 'burger' in it. He's become a vegetarian in the last couple of weeks."

"Oh, I didn't know that. Well, how about apple macaroni, then?"

"Honir thinks macaroni is slimy. He says it gives him the creeps," Loki informed her. No matter what idea she came up with, the boygod was able to name one or more students who wouldn't like it. By the time they reached the bridge, she was feeling pretty discouraged.

Heimdall greeted them in his usual friendly manner. (Not!) "Halt!" He blocked their way across the bridge. "Are those pip-purses you've got there?" he asked, eyeing the leather seed pouches around their necks.

"I don't carry a purse!" exclaimed Loki.

"A pip is another name for a seed," Idun explained. "'Pip-purses' must be Heimdall's kenning for 'seed pouches.'"

The security guard nodded. He often spoke in kennings—hyphenated-word nicknames for things. He referred to his sword as a "hurt-stick," for example, and his horn as his "noise-toot." He now pointed his hurt-stick at the *eski*. "Golden apples of youth? Also full of seeds?" He folded his muscular arms forbiddingly. "They cannot leave Asgard."

"I would never plant the seeds of my magic apples outside the walls of Asgard," Idun assured him, without bothering to explain that her magical apples couldn't be grown from seeds anyway. "And as for the seeds in our 'pip-purses,'" she went on, "they are ordinary apple seeds that I've collected walking around. They're not glittery gold like the seeds of my apples of youth. See?" She opened her "pip-purse" to show Heimdall the plain old brown seeds inside.

"Yeah." Loki showed Heimdall his pouch too. "We're off to scatter them down in Midgard to grow apples for the humans there. Our good seed-deed for the day." He laughed.

The security guard glanced at Loki with raised eyebrows. "You? Helping? Voluntarily?"

"That's right," said Loki. "Just call me Mr. Good Deed–Doer. We're taking the golden apples for when we get hungry, and so we can ride on the *eski*."

Idun couldn't believe he'd told Heimdall all this. Especially since he'd asked her not to tell anyone about their plan. Loki had always found it difficult not to boast, though.

"Want one?" Idun asked, offering a golden apple to Heimdall. "For a snack later on?"

The security guard straightened. "No snack-stractions on duty." (Which Idun figured must be his made-up word for food *dis*tractions.)

She wanted to ask him if there were any apple

recipes he was especially fond of, but he waved them on past before she could speak again. "Be back before dark," he commanded. "See you later."

"Not if we see you first," Loki joked.

Heimdall didn't laugh. Which was no surprise given his limited sense of humor. No matter. He was a cool guy in her opinion. And a superb watchman with his amazing hearing and eyesight.

Since the glistening tricolor bridge was all downhill to Midgard, and the *eski*'s runners slid well over it, Idun stood on the back tips of the runners and Loki made room for himself to crouch inside the box with the apples.

"Whee! Woo-hoo!" they both shouted, zooming lickety-split all the way down the bridge.

"Lean right!" yelled Idun sometime later as they approached the curve that would take them off the Midgard exit. Both of them leaned, causing the cart to veer in that direction. *Whoosh!* They slid down the exit ramp and off the bridge, coming to a stop seconds later on the level, snow-covered path beyond.

Laughing, they hopped off the *eski* and began to walk, pushing it ahead of them. Soon they came upon fallow farmlands with rich soil that was perfect for growing apples. Since the soil here was only lightly dusted with snow, Idun reached into her pouch and started tossing seeds right and left as they continued to walk. Following her example, Loki did the same. But every once in a while, Idun noticed, he would stop and murmur over the seeds.

"What are you saying to them?" she asked at last.

Looking charmingly embarrassed, Loki said, "It's a magic spell the gardener who took care of the grounds at my old school used to say as he worked. Bragi came up with it originally—that's when he started rhyming everything, to get over being shy."

"Shy? Bragi?"

"He used to be when we were kids. Making up all those rhymes helped him make friends, and he sort of got over it. Anyway, he made up a rhyming spell for the gardener to help things grow."

"How does it go?" Idun asked.

Loki repeated it for her:

"Grow, little seeds.

Sprout and blossom.

May whatever you bear

be healthy and awesome."

"I love it!" Idun exclaimed. How sweet of Bragi to want to help things grow at his old school! Hearing this story caused her to like him even more. And how nice of Loki to employ that spell now to help their seeds. The feeling that she was doing the right thing by encouraging him to help others strengthened. "Does the spell really work?" she asked.

Loki shrugged, grinning. "Maybe. The gardens at my school *were* awesome."

"Keep saying it, then," said Idun. "And I will too."

An hour later, Loki held his pouch upside down and shook it. "All done. I'm empty."

"Same here," Idun told him, tossing her empty pouch into the *eski*.

After tossing his in too, Loki stretched his arms high. While planting the seeds, his manner had become gentler and more open than usual. But now, though she couldn't have said what tipped her off exactly, she detected a subtle shift back toward the old "tricky" Loki.

He looked into the distance, appearing thoughtful. "You know, when Bragi and Honir and I were out skiing yesterday, I saw some apple trees in a forest not far from here. They were full of golden apples that looked exactly like the ones in your grove. Weird, huh?"

Idun shook her head firmly. "There's no other apple grove like mine."

"Yeah, you're probably right," Loki said casually. "But since we have some of your apples with us, maybe it wouldn't hurt to compare them with the ones I saw? I mean, what if someday your trees got a disease? Might be nice to have a backup source for more apples of youth, right?"

Can there really be a grove of magical apples here in Midgard? Idun wondered. Heimdall had been concerned about her special apples leaving Asgard. He and the great and powerful Odin would want to know if more magical trees existed outside of their realm. Feeling a little anxious about the notion of a competing grove or her trees getting a disease, Idun asked, "How far away is it?"

"Not far," Loki replied. Taking charge of her cart, he began to slide it, she presumed, in the direction of the other grove. "Hey, if the apples really are like yours, maybe you could claim the grove for the gods. Your apples' youth-restoring properties would have no effect on humans, so no loss to them."

Idun trotted along to keep up with him. "No loss if we offer them *new* apple groves—like the ones we just planted," she said. "If there really are more trees like mine, it would be good to know. Since only eighty-one apples can be harvested from my grove each day, another source of them would be a great find."

Loki led her to a forest at the foot of a mountain. There he paused to scoop several apples from the *eski* and put them in his pockets. "I'm getting hungry. You?" he asked as they entered the forest.

She shook her head. Before she could ask if the grove was close by now, a shadow fell over her. *Scree-ee! Scree-ee!* An eagle as big as Heimdall, with a gold crown atop its head, came swooping from the trees toward them.

"Whoa! Wait!" yelled Idun as it seized her, hooking one of its claws in the back of her *hangerock*. At the same time, it lifted the handle of her half-full *eski* with its other claw.

"Help me, Loki!" Idun shouted, reaching out to him. But that boygod was already racing away from the forest, acting like he hadn't heard her.

9
Captured

"YEAK WONBEAK GETEAK ANYEAK HELPEAK freak himeak," the eagle said to Idun as it flew higher with her and her apples. Then it laughed.

"What? I don't understand you!" she cried out.

The eagle let out an irritated huff. "Why you gods expect eagles to learn your language when you don't bother to learn ours, I'll never know. So, anyway, as I was saying—and if you'd bothered to learn eaglespeak, you'd know this already—you won't get any help from *him*. Loki owes me. He brought you here to fulfill a promise he made to me in exchange for his life yesterday."

"His life? A promise?" she said, feeling desperate as she watched the landscape pass by beneath them at tremendous speed. This must be what Freya felt when she flew in her feathered cloak, only without the terror!

"He tried to attack me after he and his two buddies hiked up to my mountaintop café yesterday," the eagle told her. "So I carried him off. We made a deal. If I let him go, he'd bring me something powerful. You."

"Me? I'm not powerful," Idun protested in confusion.

"Your apples are. Without them the gods will become old and weak. But now that I have them—and you to grow more apples from their seeds—I will stay young forevermore! See, I'm not really an eagle, but a giant in disguise. Ha-ha! I win. The gods and goddesses lose."

Idun wasn't surprised to hear that this overgrown eagle was actually a giant. Given many giants' deep dislike and distrust of goddesses and gods, they were always threatening to storm the newly rebuilt wall around Asgard. So it also wasn't surprising that the giant liked the idea of the gods becoming old and weak.

Idun's heart sank. Should she tell this eagle-giant that the apples weren't likely to have the same youthful effect on him as they did on goddesses and gods? No, then he might just drop her. Devastated by Loki's deception and betrayal, she exclaimed, "Then Loki lied to me? There never was any special Midgardian magic apple grove?"

"Is that what he told you? Ha-ha! That boy is slick," said the eagle. "And a bad seed through and through."

As she was carried farther and farther away, Idun's mortification over falling for Loki's trick grew. He'd only agreed to come with her to plant seeds because doing so had fit in with his own plans to hand her over to this eagle! "I'm starting to think you might be right," Idun murmured. She'd been such a fool! And so proud of herself for thinking she would be the one to help Loki be a better person.

Obviously Skade, Sif, and Freya had been right about Loki too. He *was* a bad seed! And now she'd put the health and well-being of her three best friends as well as the other goddesses and gods at AA in jeopardy. They were all dependent on her apples to maintain their youth!

Half an hour later, Idun's captor deposited her inside his mountaintop café. "I suppose I should properly introduce myself since you'll be my guest from here on out. Name's Thiazi," the giant-in-disguise told her. "I prefer being in eagle form to being a giant, actually. Birds just have more fun, you know? There's the flying thing. And the claws," the eagle added, flexing his. "And though I don't like to speak ill of my own kind, on the whole, giants tend to be a rather sour lot."

He was kind of right. Angerboda was a thorn in everyone's side at the academy. Even Skade, a half-giant herself, agreed that most giants were grumpy trouble-makers. Still, Odin had asked students to try to get along and give each individual a fair chance. For the most part, everyone tried to do as he'd asked.

"Um . . . I'm kind of cold. Do you mind if I sit by the fire?" Idun asked.

"Sure, go ahead," the eagle said, parking her half-full *eski* in a corner. "Sit wherever you like."

Even though Idun was super tired and scared, she carefully studied the room, looking for possible ways to escape or weapons. Or something that would help her warn her friends. Like maybe smoke signals? Unfortunately, the firepit was only full of warm coals at the moment, but she would save the idea for later.

Idun pulled out a chair at one of the café's four round tables and sat. The café was pretty bare of decoration, though there were a couple of posters on its walls. One was a map of the nine worlds. A big *X* had been marked on the border between Midgard and Jotunheim. The words YOU ARE HERE had been printed next to the *X* in large block letters.

The other poster had the word WARNING! written at the top of it. Beneath the word was a picture of the head of an eagle in profile with a magnifying glass held up to its eye. MY EAGLE EYE IS WATCHING YOU! read the words below the picture. Not exactly friendly!

Extending a claw toward Idun's *eski*, Thiazi snagged one of the golden apples of youth. Clacking his beak as he munched on the apple, he told her, "I can't wait to add your apples to new recipes I'll be developing."

"Ooh! I would love to help you make those for your customers," said Idun. And for the Valhallateria, too, she thought to herself. If she ever got free, that was.

"Ha! No way. My secret recipes will stay just that. Secret. I'll tell you the names of some, though, just to whet your appetite. Of course, my café is already famous for my oxtail soup. Soon I'll add apple crumble, stuffed apples, apple peel soup . . . I could go on and on. Since Loki visited yesterday, I've come up with endless ideas," said the talkative Thiazi. "However, my customers will never actually get a chance to eat anything I prepare because I devour everything I cook before they can taste even one bite. Joke's on them!" He cracked up laughing.

Huh? This eagle-giant was decidedly cuckoo! "What will you do when my *eski* is empty? You can't keep me here and get more golden apples, you know!" she protested. "Their seeds won't grow more magic apple trees. My grove in Asgard is the only one in all the nine worlds. And I am the only one who can pick the apples."

Thiazi just laughed. "Not a problem. You Norse gods and goddesses are powerful, but you're not immortal. Within a couple of days, Loki and all the others will have aged so much that they'll be too weak—or too *dead*—to try to stop me from doing whatever I want. It'll be a snap for me to fly you to the grove to pick more apples every morning."

"What if I won't pick more apples?" Idun challenged.

Thiazi glowered at her. "You'd better. Or you'll grow old just like the rest of your friends."

Clasping her hands together, Idun leaned forward in her chair. "Please, I have another idea," she begged, as worried for her friends as for herself. "If you'll return me to Asgard, I promise I'll give you a share of the apples I pick every day from now on. Forever."

"Yeah, right!" Thiazi said, clacking his beak. "Like Odin would ever let you do that!"

"I'll convince him," Idun said, really hoping she could. "C'mon. Be a good guy!"

"Like how you gods and goddesses were good guys to Ymir?" he scoffed. He was obviously one of those giants who forever harbored ill will toward Asgard because the gods had helped create the nine worlds out of their ancestor long ago. Deaf to her pleas, Thiazi told her, "I'm flying off to the sea to go fishing. I'll be back before dusk, and we'll make apple-baked fish with oxtail gravy. Sound good?"

He was leaving her alone? Idun perked up. "Sure! I'll straighten things up around here and maybe cut up any ingredients you'll need."

"Nice try," said Thiazi. "But if I left you here in the main part of the café, you might find a way to escape." So saying, he herded her into a small pantry full of cooking stuff at the back of his café. Then, after giving her a single one of her own golden apples to keep her from aging, he shut the pantry door and turned a key in the lock.

"Wait! Please, you have to let me go!" She banged on the door for a long time, but to no avail. That evil eagle had flown the coop, er, café.

10
Where's Idun?

MEANWHILE, BACK AT THE BRANCHWAY, IT
was lunchtime and Bragi was getting concerned. "Any-
body seen Idun?" he asked her friends when they crossed
paths on the way to the Valhallateria.

"No, we were just going to ask you the same thing,"
said Freya. "We haven't seen her since before breakfast."

Bragi's eyebrows rose. "She didn't say what she was
doing today?" he asked Freya, falling into step with her,
Sif, and Skade.

"Only that she was off to tend her apple grove first thing," Freya told him. "Which is what she does most mornings."

"We were just there, though," Sif added. "She wasn't anywhere around."

"But she must have been there earlier because the apples on about half the trees had been picked," said Skade.

As Bragi watched, Freya pulled her amazing walnut-size teardrop-shaped jewel from one of the pouches that hung around her neck. "Tell me, Brising, where is Idun? Is she in danger?" she asked her magical jewel. After listening carefully, she repeated the jewel's reply that only she could hear:

> "Her exact location I cannot see,
> But here is the vision that comes to me.
> Shelves of spices, pots, and pans.
> And Idun, a girl who's hatching plans."

"That sounds like she could be in the V's kitchen!" Skade exclaimed.

The group picked up their pace along the broad path. Bragi could already see the Valhallateria's gold-thatched roof shining through Yggdrasil's branches ahead. He wasn't so sure they'd find Idun there, though. Something felt off about all this. "Why would she leave half the apples unpicked?"

Sif shrugged a shoulder. "Maybe she got interrupted?"

"Yeah, someone might've come along and needed something," said Skade.

"She's always helping out friends with stuff, you know?" added Freya. She cocked her head at Bragi. "That's why we wondered if you'd seen her. Because you guys were talking together yesterday, acting like *friends*."

Bragi's cheeks warmed at Freya's emphasis on the word "friends." Had these girls guessed that he was crushing on Idun? Had Idun herself figured it out? His cheeks heated even more. Since Freya was the girlgoddess of love (as well as beauty), she probably had a sixth sense about these things. Whatever! This wasn't the time to worry about stuff like that. They'd arrived at the Valhallateria and needed to find out if Idun was in trouble.

Moving ahead, he pulled on one of the V-shaped door handles and then stepped aside to let the girls enter first. He had noticed this was something Odin did for his wife, Ms. Frigg, and he thought it was kind of cool. Plus, he admired Principal Odin enough to copy stuff he did like this.

"Maybe she's been in the V all this time. She could have delivered half of her apples and then stayed to talk to the Valkyries," Sif said hopefully.

Bragi nodded. "Yeah, maybe." But a quick scan of the V's dining area, which was beginning to fill with students, showed that Idun wasn't there.

"Let's check the kitchen," Freya suggested. Crossing the room, they moved past the apple juice–spouting Heidrun.

Just as they were about to enter the kitchen's double doors, a voice from within called out a warning: "Door!"

Scrambling, all four students managed to leap aside. They barely missed being mowed down by a Valkyrie exiting the kitchen. She was bearing two huge trays, one balanced on each of her raised palms. Seeing Freya and the others, she wavered, almost losing one of the trays before righting it.

"Ooh! Careful. Watch where you're going!" she cautioned before zooming out into the room full of hungry students.

"Sorry!" Sif called after her.

Copying the Valkyrie's warning, Skade yelled "Door!" to any other kitchen workers within earshot. Then the four students pushed safely through the double doors and into the kitchen.

Bragi studied the hive of activity inside. Valkyries flitted around, busily cooking over stoves, putting things into or taking things out of ovens, juggling platters and pots of various foods. Magical spoons, unassisted by anyone's hands, were stirring pots while magical knives raced up and down a line of cutting boards, chopping up fruits and vegetables. Despite the seeming chaos, it was easy to see that Idun wasn't here. But maybe she'd been in the kitchen earlier?

"Excuse us!" Freya called over the din.

A Valkyrie with bright red hair glanced up. Flapping her wings, she flew eagerly over to the group. "I know you girls. You're Idun's friends, right? Did you bring her golden apples?"

The four of them shook their heads. "We were just going to ask if she'd delivered any of them here today like usual," Sif said. "We can't find her."

The Valkyrie's shoulders slumped, and she sighed. "Ymir's soup bowl! No! We're all out and we need more. Used the last of yesterday's apples in this morning's turnovers, so—"

Before she could finish whatever she'd been about to

the turnovers we served at breakfast, as well as the juice, were all made from regular apples."

Skade frowned. "So *nothing* we ate at breakfast today came from Idun's apples of youth?"

"'Fraid not," the red-haired Valkyrie said with a sigh. "I hope that girlgoddess shows up soon with today's crop. Or else."

Bragi was about to ask exactly what that meant, when another Valkyrie flew up to explain. "Idun can only harvest eighty-one apples each day from her grove, a rather limited supply."

The other Valkyrie nodded. "So we always use a mix of her magic apples and ordinary ones for every recipe requiring apples. Normally, that means a ratio of one part apples of youth to ten parts regular apples."

"I never knew that," Bragi said in surprise as both Valkyries flew off back to their work. The second Valkyrie had brought a tray of snacks, so he and the friends began munching as they spoke.

say, Freya interrupted her with a gasp. "Oh no! I skipped the turnovers at breakfast today. I just had oatmeal!" She hurried over to where some shiny pots dangled from hooks on a rack fixed to the ceiling. Looking upward, she stared at her reflection in the polished metal bottom of a large frying pan as if it were a mirror.

Seemed like a strange time to be checking her appearance when she was worried about her friend, Bragi thought, but whatever. Girls were pretty much mystery to him.

With a worried look on her face, Sif glanced at Freya and then back at the Valkyrie. "Well apple juice hasn't stopped flowing from she noted.

The Valkyrie nodded. "True, but that from Idun's apples. We tried a new re turnovers this morning, and as I sta paused here and flicked a look studying her reflection. "We ac

"Me neither," said Sif.

"Same here," said Skade. "The power of Idun's apples must be superstrength if a one-to-ten ratio is enough to keep us all young."

"I wonder how long the youthful effects last if—" Bragi started to say. But before he could finish with *the supply of Idun's apples runs out*, Freya gave a yelp.

All this time she had continued to gaze at herself in the shiny frying pan's bottom, but now she whirled around to face him and her friends. "My hair!" she cried out, a horrified look on her face. "It's turning gray!"

When they hurried over to look, the girls gasped and Bragi gaped. Because it was true. Freya's normally long pale-blond hair was slowly turning a dull gray. She tugged on Skade's and Sif's arms and stuck her face close to theirs so that they were almost nose to nose. "Quick, look at me. Am I getting wrinkles?"

"I . . . I don't know," said Skade, squinting at Freya's

face. "Something has happened to my eyesight. I think I need glasses!" Since she was half-goddess (besides being half-giant), she depended on Idun's apples to stay youthful too!

"What did you say?" asked Sif, cupping her ear. "My hearing's gone bad."

"Uh-oh. This is not good," Bragi told the girls. "Do the math. Last night's dinner was around six, and it's nearly noon now. That means it's been close to eighteen hours since we last ate anything made with Idun's special apples. Apparently, that's about how long their youth-restoring effects last. If we don't find Idun fast and get her picking apples in her grove again, Asgard Academy is going to turn into a retirement home."

"What? Why would you want to 'knit her pickled apples in a stove'?" asked Sif, cupping a hand around one ear again. "I didn't know you could knit. And why in a stove?"

While Skade explained loudly to Sif what he'd actually said, Bragi rubbed his chin, thinking hard about where Idun could possibly be. "Whaaa?" he said in surprise. "My chin! It's all prickly. I'm growing a beard!"

He and Loki had been wishing they could grow beards. Heimdall had told them they shouldn't be in too big of a hurry to grow up, though. Who knew that warning would turn out to be prophetic? Cool as a beard was, he wasn't ready to get old. He had only just gotten his first crush on a girl!

Toot! Toot! Toooot! Just then three long, low blasts sounded from a distant horn. "Heimdall's emergency signal!" Bragi exclaimed. "We're being summoned to Gladsheim."

"I think I can guess what the emergency is," said Freya. "Gray hair and wrinkles! We can't be the only ones getting old too soon around here."

The four friends dashed from the kitchen and through the eating area to join other students fleeing outside. Once they'd funneled out through the

V's main doors, they made their way along branch-ways and fernways. Gladsheim Hall's silver-thatched roof shone up ahead in the pale sunshine that peeked through Yggdrasil's branches and leaves.

Since the apples of youth didn't affect them, the appearances of human, elf, giant, and dwarf students and teachers hadn't changed. However, everyone was gawking at the young goddesses and gods, shocked at how suddenly they were aging. Some moved more slowly than usual with shuffling steps, or they were hobbling along with walking sticks.

"Ow! Watch where you're going!" Skade said, bumping into a tree and mistaking it for another student.

"Excuse us," Bragi said to the tree. Then he nudged Skade around it before she could realize her mistake and get embarrassed.

Minutes later, they all entered Gladsheim Hall.

11
Gladsheim Gathering

F**ROM BESIDE BRAGI, SIF GASPED. "LOOK!** It's Odin and Ms. Frigg!"

On a raised platform at the front of Gladsheim Hall stood an elderly god and goddess. Bragi's eyes widened in surprise, because these two coprincipals of the academy had aged almost beyond recognition!

Once the most awe-inspiring, powerful god of all, Odin was now bent and frail. Draupnir, his magical gold arm-ring, hung loose around his elbow now as he leaned on a walking stick. No, wait. That wasn't a walking stick, but Gungnir, his magical spear. The spear was famous for always finding its mark when thrown, but Odin probably lacked the strength to even lift it now!

As usual, he wore a black patch over one eye. His single good eye, which had always been startlingly clear and bright blue, was now milky and pale. And gone was Ms. Frigg's thick and fashionably styled blond hair, as well as her straight-backed, graceful figure. Her hair had become wispy and white, and her skin practically hung from her bones.

Everyone watched as the pair lowered themselves, groaning, to sit upon two carved majestic thrones. *Caw! Caw!* Two large black ravens flew into the hall through an open window and landed on Odin's now-bony shoulders.

Squinting his single good eye, Odin surveyed the crowd. Everyone quieted as he began to speak. "As you've probably figured out by now, Idun is missing!" he called out in a croaky voice. "We must find her and her apples before it's too late. If anyone has any information that might help . . ."

"I do!" a voice announced from the back of the room. Bragi and the rest of those gathered in the hall turned to see Heimdall. Gasps swept the room. Because the school watchman had aged too! He was practically bald now, with a large paunchy stomach that hung over his belt and strained at the buttons of his uniform.

"I spoke to her on the Bifrost Bridge this morning," Heimdall went on as he made his way through the crowd to stand before the thrones. He turned sideways so that he could address both the coprincipals and the crowd at once. "She had her *eski* with her," he said in a voice loud enough for everyone to hear. "It was half full. Said she was off to scatter apple seeds—ordinary ones—down in Midgard." He paused, then asked dramatically, "Guess who was going with her?"

"Loki?" several voices called out at once. Other voices joined them, till his name became a roar. "LOKI!"

159

Bragi groaned. Since his friend and roomie was usually at the heart of any trouble at Asgard Academy, it was a fair guess that he was involved somehow.

"You got it!" Heimdall boomed.

An angry murmur rose from the crowd. Even Angerboda, who usually acted like she was crushing on Loki, joined in, living up to the "anger" part of her name.

Bragi felt angry too. This time it seemed Loki had gone too far. What had he done with Idun?

"Go, everyone! Search for Idun and Loki and bring them here!" Odin ordered. Though he might be frail, he hadn't lost his ability to command. His magical ravens, Hugin and Munin, hopped up and down on his shoulders.

"What did he say?" asked Sif as everyone stampeded toward the exit (though not as quickly as they might once have done in their former youth). Bragi watched Freya lean close to Sif to fill her in on what had been said, but after that he lost track of the girls as they were swept up in the surging crowd.

Caw! Caw! Just as he reached Gladsheim's doors, Bragi looked up to see Hugin and Munin flap out of a high window. They'd be searching too. After all, part of their job was to fly out over the world daily to gather what news they could. When they returned to perch on Odin's shoulders, they would whisper whatever they'd seen and heard into his ears. Hopefully soon that news would be that Idun, and Loki as well, were safe!

As everyone left the hall and spread out to search for the missing students, Bragi wound up next to Honir. "What do you think is going on?" Honir asked him.

"Idun would never ignore her responsibility to supply the V with her golden apples," Bragi replied worriedly. "Something must've happened to stop her."

Honir twirled the ends of the handlebar mustache he now sported and nodded. "Yeah, something named Loki."

"Seems like it," Bragi agreed. "Let's search for them together," he suggested. "We can start in Midgard, since Heimdall said that's where they were heading." He glanced up at the overcast sky. The temperature had fallen since morning and soon it would be snowing again. He pulled his mittens and hat from the pocket of his tunic and put them on. Then he wrapped his cloak more tightly about him.

"Okay," said Honir. His lanky frame shook with a shiver. "Brr," he said, blowing on his fingers. "I'm c-c-cold."

"Put on your mittens and hat," Bragi told him.

Most students wouldn't need to be told to do that, but Honir was Honir. It probably hadn't occurred to him that he could make himself less cold.

Honir stuck his hands into his tunic pockets. As his fingers searched inside them, a puzzled look came over his face. "They're not h-h-here," he said at last.

"You probably left them in our room," Bragi said. "We can stop by the dorm and get them before we go down to Midgard."

"Y-y-yeah," Honir replied through chattering teeth.

The two boygods detoured to Breidablik Hall and in no time were passing through the main room with its communal firepit and collection of tables and stools. They made a beeline for their room, one of eighteen sleeping pods of various sizes that were spaced all around the edge of the round-shaped common area.

"Be quick," Bragi said as he and Honir pushed in through the door of the sleeping pod they shared with Loki. "If you can't find your hat and mittens in your closet, I've got extras in mine you can borrow."

Inside their pod, both boys came to an abrupt halt, eyes bugging out in surprise. "Loki?" they said at the exact same time.

Apparently unaware that everyone was out hunting for him, the boygod was lying in his podbed, which was basically a hammock, munching on an apple and reading a comic book. He did a double take when he looked up and saw Bragi and Honir.

"Whoa!" he said. Then he laughed. "Look at you two. Talk about a hairy situation! Is that stick-on beard hair?"

Bragi ignored this comment. Seeing that Loki looked as young as always, his eyes narrowed. "Is that one of Idun's golden apples you're eating?" He stepped closer to Loki's podbed. At the same time, he looked over his shoulder at Honir and silently mouthed the words *Follow my lead*. Luckily, the often-clueless boy seemed to catch Bragi's drift, and he stepped closer to Loki too.

Loki swung his legs over the side of his podbed to sit on the edge of it. "Yeah, I think so," he said, sounding a little wary now. After polishing off what remained of the apple in two quick bites, he rose to toss its core in the nearby trash can.

With a nod toward Honir, Bragi shouted, "Now! Get him!" In a flash, he slipped behind Loki and hooked a hand under each of his armpits. Meanwhile, Honir stooped and grabbed hold of Loki's ankles. Together they lifted and carried the squirming and protesting boygod in the direction of Gladsheim Hall. It wasn't easy, since Bragi and Honir were both missing the usual youthful effects of consuming Idun's magic apples. They moved slowly, huffing and puffing.

"Where's Idun?" Bragi demanded of Loki along the way. "What did you do with her?"

"Who, me? Nothing! I don't know what you're talking about," Loki replied. "What makes you think I'd know where your *girlfriend* is?"

"Idun's not my girlfriend," blustered Honir, mis-understanding.

Ignoring this, Bragi said to Loki, "Everyone's looking for her. Heimdall said you both went down to Midgard this morning to plant apple seeds."

A look of guilty surprise darted across Loki's face. "Oh, yeah. We did do that," he admitted. "But then we came back. She's probably in her dorm room over in Vingolf Hall. If you'll put me down, we can all go see."

"Okay," Honir said agreeably.

"No! Don't let him go," Bragi warned in the nick of time. "We have to keep hold of him, remember? Or he else he'll shape-shift and get away." That was the way shape-shifting magic worked, as Loki well knew. As long as anyone touched him with so much as a fingertip, he couldn't change shape, but once they let go, shifting would be easy.

"Oh, right," said Honir.

Seeing that they were onto him, Loki began to twist, turn, and yell vigorously in an effort to get free. Hearing the commotion, other students came running, including Skade, Sif, and the mighty boygod Thor. Thor and Skade grabbed on to Loki too, just in case. Bragi was glad, because in his new "old" state, Loki seemed way heavy and strong.

"Idun isn't in our dorm room. We just checked," Skade told Loki flatly when he insisted again that she was probably there.

"We just pecked? I didn't peck anything," Sif said, looking confused. When Skade repeated what she'd actually said more loudly, Sif nodded. "Oh, right. *Checked*. She's not there. And she wouldn't just go off somewhere without picking and delivering her apples to the V first."

Bragi nodded in agreement.

"That's right!" several other students chimed in to say.

By now they'd carried Loki all the way to the doors of Gladsheim Hall. Honir and the others let go of Loki's feet, allowing him to stand, but Thor kept hold of his arms. Though Thor wasn't as superstrong as before he'd aged, he still had more muscles than anyone else around.

"Last chance before you face Odin," Bragi warned Loki, nodding toward the hall door. "Spill your guts. Where's Idun?"

As if to make this threat even clearer, Skade added, "If you don't tell us right now where to find her, we're taking you inside. Where Odin and Ms. Frigg await."

Loki cringed. "Okay, okay," he said at last. "I'll tell you what happened." Quickly he explained about the deal he'd made yesterday with the eagle-giant Thiazi in order to gain his release.

"I knew there must have been a reason he suddenly let go of you and that ladle in midair!" Bragi exclaimed. "But I can't believe you let him kidnap Idun just to save your own skin."

"I can!" several students called out, including Thor, Sif, and Skade.

Just then, falcon-Freya soared down from the sky. Her shape-shifting feather cloak drew oohs and aahs from those who hadn't seen it in use till now. Once she landed, she removed the cloak and laid it over her arm, then put on her red wool cloak, which Sif had been holding for her.

"Oh, good, you found Loki," Freya announced breathlessly. She sagged against the hall door, looking totally winded. "Just got back from flying over Asgard to look for Idun and him from above. But I came up empty." Eyeing Loki, she demanded, "So where is she?"

Loki shrugged helplessly. "Wherever Thiazi took her."

"Thiazi?" Freya repeated.

As the situation was explained to Freya, Loki insisted that he'd had no choice about what he'd done. "Yeah, I probably shouldn't have lost my temper and hit that giant with the soup ladle. But Thiazi would never have let me go without a promise that I'd bring Idun and her apples to him. If it's a choice between me or someone else, of course I'll save myself," he said, as if this were the only reasonable course of action.

"Yes, *you* would," Freya agreed irritably. "But think about this. Your choice has doomed a great many of us at the academy, including you! Because without Idun and her apples, we're all going to age quickly and die."

"Hmm. That *is* a problem," Loki admitted. "So what's your solution?"

"Why do *we* have to fix *your* mess?" demanded Skade, going nose to nose with him.

Echoing Skade, others began to grumble. "Yeah. Why should we?"

To rein things in before they could get out of hand, Bragi called for quiet. "Let's check that café. Thiazi is probably holding Idun captive there. Someone needs to rescue her. And fast!"

"Thor? Couldn't you go after Thiazi and bonk him on the head with Mjollnir?" Sif suggested.

Looking a little embarrassed, Thor admitted, "Mjollnir is back at my pod. That hammer is heavy, and I'm too weak to lift it right now. Someone else will have to rescue her."

At this, everyone looked at Loki. "What? Me?" he asked. "You expect *me* to go after her?"

They all just glared at him. "It's your fault Thiazi's got her," Sif pointed out.

"Besides, look at us," Skade said, motioning to herself and the gray-haired students around her. "Look how tired out Freya got just flying a little way. We aren't fit enough to go. Not at the rate we're aging. And that's your fault too! So get going!"

"Or would you rather discuss this with Odin? Huh, Loki?" Bragi jerked his head toward Gladsheim's double-doors again.

Odin could be pretty terrifying when angry—even an old Odin. So it was no surprise when Loki quickly replied, "Okay, I'll go." There was a resigned look in his eyes as he glanced around at the other students. However, his eyes lit up when they settled on the feather cloak still draped over Freya's arm. "Only I'll need to borrow Freya's shape-shifting cloak."

"Ha!" said Freya. "No way. You can travel just as

fast wearing your magic yellow racing shoes."

"True," said Loki, "but then Thiazi would see me coming. To have any chance at rescuing Idun, I need to go in disguise."

"But you can shape-shift into anything you want," Freya argued.

"Yeah, but Thiazi's mountaintop café is quite a journey," Loki told her. "It takes a lot of energy to hold a shape for such a long period of time." He hesitated a moment before going on. "And it's also likely that Idun will be mad at me if and when I find her."

"Duh, you think?" Skade burst out.

"Drink what?" asked Sif, cupping her ear in confusion.

Loki ignored them. "So anyway, if I wear your feather cloak, Freya, I can fool Idun into thinking I'm you. She'll probably let me rescue her no questions asked."

Freya frowned at him, frustrated. "I wish I could just go myself."

Loki shrugged. "Face it, you oldie moldies." He waved toward the crowd, whose gray hair and wrinkles were multiplying as fast as the snowflakes that were beginning to fall. "You're too weak and slow pokey to make it all the way there and back. I'm the only one youthful enough to go."

"So it would seem," Bragi said resentfully. He understood Freya's and Thor's frustration. If he thought he had the strength and stamina to rescue Idun himself, he'd have volunteered in a heartbeat to don Freya's cloak and go after her. He studied Loki for a minute and a new thought occurred to him. "Have you got a stash of Idun's apples hidden somewhere nearby?" he snapped. Even just a slice or two of one her apples would give him and a few others the strength they'd need to effect a rescue.

"Sorry," Loki told him. "You just saw me eat the last one. There are more on the trees, but we all know they'll wither if we try to pick them. C'mon, if we wait much longer, I'll start to age too. And then what will we do? Ticktock, time's a-wasting. Cloak, please." He held an arm out to Freya.

Finally persuaded, she said, "I guess we'll have to trust you. Just remember, you need Idun back here safe as much as we all do." Reluctantly she handed Loki her cloak.

"Help! Thief!" the cloak cried out when it realized that the person holding it wasn't Freya.

"It's okay," Freya reassured it. "I'm letting Loki borrow you, but just for a few hours." She fixed Loki with a stern look. "If you so much as bend one of my cloak's feathers, I'll shred your yellow racing shoes—and you— to bits."

A look of alarm flitted across Loki's face, but then he grinned. "Warning noted, Ms. Graya. I mean Freya," he told her, cracking up.

Freya rolled her eyes.

With things decided, Thor released Loki's arms at

last. Instantly Loki threw Freya's cloak across his shoulders. Just as it had with Freya, the cloak quickly tightened around his body, wings opening up from its sides and beginning to flap.

Watching falcon-Loki take to the sky and vanish into the thickly swirling snowflakes, Bragi hoped they'd done the right thing. And that Idun was okay.

12
Imprisoned

WITH A FEELING OF UTTER DEFEAT, IDUN sank to the pantry floor after the eagle-giant locked her in alone. She was too upset to feel hungry, even though she'd only had two apples to eat since last night's dinner. Tears of self-pity welled in her eyes, but she angrily wiped them away.

"Just because your plan to help Loki do a good deed didn't work, doesn't mean you can't save yourself!" she admonished herself out loud. Sitting with her back against the door, she deliberately took bites of the single magic golden apple Thiazi had given her to keep up her strength. With each bite, however, her worry escalated.

Crunch. What was happening to her friends and all the others at the academy who depended on her apples to stay youthful? Since she hadn't delivered any apples today, the Valhallateria kitchen would be running low on them by dinnertime.

Munch. The youth-restoring effects of her apples would start to wear off after eighteen hours. And then goddesses and gods would begin to age quickly. She'd expected that she and Loki would be back before lunch to finish picking apples for the V kitchen. Oh, how she regretted trusting him now!

Crunch. Crunch. How long would it be before her friends realized she was missing?

Nibble. Nibble. Crunch. When everyone finally did notice she was gone, would they know where to look for her? Loki wasn't likely to tell them what had happened.

"Yeah, because you set up this whole trick, Loki!" she grumped aloud into the surrounding silence as she sat in the dim pantry.

She stared at the half-eaten apple she held, thinking hard. Bragi and Honir had to be the "two companions" Thiazi had referred to when he'd mentioned Loki's visit. Those three boygods had gone hiking and skiing together yesterday. She doubted very much that Bragi and Honir knew anything about the "deal" Loki had struck with Thiazi, though. Loki would have been too embarrassed and secretive to tell them.

Crunch. Crunch. Crunch. If anyone asked Heimdall, he'd recall her going off with Loki to plant apple seeds in Midgard. Still, that information alone wouldn't help her friends find her. No, she couldn't count on others coming to her rescue. It was up to *her* to gain her freedom. But how?

Suddenly she perked up a bit. She'd eaten her apple down to the core, and now she was feeling its restorative powers. Her brain jerked out of scared-and-hopeless mode and into come-up-with-a-plan-to-get-out-of-here mode. She'd been all about helping others lately. Well, now she needed to help herself—by finding a way to escape! And actually, that would help others, too. Because they needed her to pick the apples of youth to keep them healthy.

She tossed her apple core in a high arc, aiming for an empty mixing bowl on one of the shelves across from where she sat. *Score!* The little victory brightened her spirits further. Jumping up, she pushed aside the curtain over a small, high window so that enough light entered the room for her to see fairly well. Quickly she began rummaging through the supplies on the shelves, seeking anything that might aid in an escape.

There were cloth bags of flour and sugar, dried veggies, and many jars of spices. But how could these help? Maybe, upon Thiazi's return, she could heave a big load of flour at him as soon as he opened the door? She might be able to blind that eagle-eyed giant long enough to dash past him. Would it work?

"Doubtful," she murmured to a spoon she'd picked up. "He'll just fly after me and recapture me as soon as he recovers. Too risky a plan, don't you think?" she asked the spoon. She wiggled it up and down, pretending it had responded with a nod in the affirmative. "Right. So I'll keep that as plan B. Now I just need to figure out a plan A. Something more likely to succeed."

The minutes ticked by as Idun examined other items on the pantry shelves and mulled over conversations with Loki that had led up to her capture. At dinner last night, he'd told her what a coincidence it was that she'd wanted to talk to him because he'd wanted to talk to her too. *Grr.* His sitting with her had been no "coincidence" for sure. All along he'd been plotting to find a way to get her out to that forest and into Thiazi's clutches!

It stunk to realize that Loki had only agreed to scatter apple seeds in Midgard because doing so would help with his *own* plan. "I totally fell for his trick!" she told a dragon-head-shaped oven mitt she found in the drawer of a sideboard.

Slipping her hand into it, she pretended the mitt was a puppet. "True," she made the dragon mitt say, while bending her fingers open and closed to make it "speak." "The fact that Loki was so easy to convince should have caused alarm bells to go off," the mitt-puppet chided her. "But instead, you allowed yourself to believe he really did want to change."

"Hey, don't worry about my feelings," Idun told the dragon mitt. "Just tell it like it is."

The makeshift puppet (in reality her own self) continued its scolding. "And then when he flattered you, suggesting you take your 'scrumptious' apples to eat on the trip, you totally fell for that, too!"

Idun had had enough. "Oh, hush up, you dumb mitt-mouth dragon," she told it. She shook her hand till it slipped off. *Whack!* It knocked aside a stack of large paper-thin sheets of tree bark. There was writing on them. Ingredients. Instructions. Thiazi's recipes! Maybe if she threatened to burn them in his firepit, he'd let her go. Risky idea, though. She'd keep that as plan C.

As she eyed the jars of spices on a shelf she'd passed over earlier, a new idea came to her. She picked up a spice jar at random and dashed it to the floor to shatter it. The smell of cinnamon wafted to her nose. *Mmm.* Using a long-handled spoon, she carefully rummaged through the cinnamon-covered glass shards to find a long glass splinter.

"You ought to work," Idun murmured to it. Tearing a piece of cloth from a flour bag, she wrapped it over her fingers to keep from cutting herself as she picked up the shard. Back by the door again, she kneeled and carefully tried to push the shard through the keyhole.

"*Drat!* Too *fat*," she muttered to the shard. Realizing that she'd rhymed like Bragi, she smiled. Thinking of him and her friends made her even more determined to escape.

She could see now that even if the shard had fit, it would have been too short for her to hold on to once it was inside the lock. Turning, she now found herself eye level with a low shelf she'd overlooked earlier. On it lay a bundle of thin sticks—skewers for threading cubes of meat and veggies for grilling. Perfect!

Excitement shot through her. After pulling one of the skewers from the bundle, she poked it into the lock. She wiggled the stick around a bit and then pushed. *Clack!* Something inside the lock gave way. *Success!*

Idun opened the door and stepped out of the pantry into the café. She'd done it. She was free! She took a few steps toward her *eski*, then paused. Thiazi's recipes! They could prove useful. In a flash, she dashed back inside for them and then tossed them into her *eski* ato' the remaining golden apples.

Seconds later she was riding on the back of her *e.* its runners taking her smoothly down the mount; side. It was snowing heavily now, and she guessed f

183

the amount of filtered light overhead that it was late afternoon. Just as she reached the bottom of the mountain, she heard the shrill cry of a bird somewhere overhead. *EeYEE!* She froze as the *eski* slowed to a halt. Was Thiazi returning?

Wait! That call had sounded more like a . . . a falcon! Her eyes searched the skies. At first she couldn't see the bird clearly because of the falling snow. But then it dove lower and she saw that it definitely wasn't an eagle. She'd been right. It *was* a falcon! Her heart lifted. Daring to hope, she shouted out, "Freya? Here I am!"

Her forest-green cloak stood out against the bright white snow, but from a distance it might make her look like a tree. So just in case the bird really was falcon-Freya but unable to hear her, Idun waved her arms and jumped up and down too.

At once the falcon gave another shrill cry and headed straight for her.

13
A Nutty Idea

"FREYA! I'M SO GLAD TO SEE YOU!" IDUN exclaimed as the falcon landed in front of her. But instead of shrugging off its feather cloak, the falcon regarded her with one beady eye and whispered some magic words under its breath. Quick as a wink, Idun was transformed into a nut! An acorn to be precise. *Whoa!* She'd had no idea Freya could do that!

The falcon picked her up in one claw and clasped

her *eski* in its other. And then they were off, winging toward Asgard as fast as the bird could go.

"Freya!" Idun called out, relieved to discover she could speak even in nut form. "When did you learn how to shape-shift a girlgoddess into a nut? Smart of you to make me lighter to carry, but I'm glad you didn't transform my *eski*, too. That might've damaged my apples!" Unfortunately, her voice was now so high-pitched and tiny that the falcon seemed unable to hear her over its own beating wings and shrill cries.

But if the falcon cloak was mine, I could have flown away from Thiazi on my own without Freya's help. The thought had floated into her head, unbidden. Even after everything, it seemed Idun still couldn't let go of the injustice of losing such an awesome cloak.

The snowfall let up as they sailed above Midgard. Though clasped in the falcon's claw, Idun was nevertheless able to see out between its talons. Through breaks in the clouds she looked down on the farms and villages they passed over. They hadn't been flying for more than a few minutes, however, when a sharp cry came from behind them. *Scree-ee!*

"Ymir's eyeballs!" Idun cried out in her tiny, nutty voice. "Thiazi!" Still wearing his crown, that huge regal eagle was chasing them.

A wave of despair washed over Idun. In a nutshell, she felt doomed! "Faster, if you can!" she urged, even though falcon-Freya didn't seem to hear her tiny voice. Falcons were usually faster than eagles, but Freya hadn't been a falcon for long. She'd only used the feather cloak a few times and probably needed more flying practice. "C'mon, Freya, you can do it!" acorn-Idun urged. But as the stronger and much larger eagle drew closer, a fatigued falcon-Freya faltered.

"Look! Up ahead!" Idun yelled as loud as she could. "See that huge pile of wood shavings and sticks outside the wall around Asgard? I bet Odin and everyone else built it. They must be trying to help us somehow!" Seeming to hear her at last, the falcon rallied. Putting on a final burst of speed, it headed for the wall.

Odin looked terrible, Idun saw as they swooped lower. Still, as saggy and weak as he'd become, he had obviously been watching their flight toward Asgard from Hlidskjalf, his high seat in one of Yggdrasil's tip-top branches overlooking all nine worlds. *But how is the pile of sticks and shavings outside the wall supposed to help?* she wondered.

By itself, the wall did a great job of keeping Asgard safe from enemies. After it was recently repaired, the Bifrost Bridge—guarded by Heimdall and rotating shifts of students—became the only way in by foot. But both the wall and the bridge could be flown over.

"Light the pile!" Odin cried out as they neared.

"Eh? Fight the smile?" Idun heard someone call out in confusion. "Why would we need to do that? Nobody here feels like smiling!"

Some of the students must be so old now that they couldn't hear well, she realized. They were in desperate need of her apples of youth! Luckily, someone managed to strike flint and spark a fire just as she and the falcon dove over the wall.

Whoosh! Flames shot up the very instant they were safely past. Hot on their tail, Thiazi the eagle-giant tried to pull back in time to dodge the fire. But without success. *Pzzt!*

"Yee-OWCH!" he yelled. The fire had singed his tail feathers! While twisting his head to blow on them, he plunged head over claws toward the ground outside the wall. At the very last moment, he somehow managed to pull up. Glimpsing Thor atop the wall, and figuring (wrongly, since he could no longer lift it) that Mjollnir must be close by, the eagle-giant decided he'd been beaten. *Scree-ee!* Turning tail, he winged off in the direction of his mountaintop café, muttering incomprehensible eaglespeak curses as he flew away.

189

Suddenly Idun felt the talons around her open. "Freya! Wait!" But acorn-Idun was already falling through the air. *Plunk!* After hitting the soft, snowy ground, she dizzily rolled down a slight slope.

When she came to a stop and looked up, a big squirrel face was staring down at her. *Ratatosk!* "Hello, little nut," he said, scooping her up. "How did you escape my bag?" Having mistaken her for one of his message acorns, he was about to toss her into his knapsack.

"No! Stop! I'm Idun!" she yelled in her tiny voice.

"Wha—?" Opening his paw, the squirrel stared at her in surprise. Beyond him, the falcon landed on the ground with her *eski.*

At that same moment three grandmotherly looking women just beyond Ratatosk came shuffling up to the falcon. One wore violet boots like the ones Skade had bought at the mall. Was this really her?

Idun's little acorn-eyes widened when she realized

that these *had* to be her friends. They had aged so much, however, that they were practically unrecognizable! Skade's boots were a dead giveaway, though. And Sif's hair, being metallic instead of real, remained as golden as ever. Freya was recognizable too, since she still wore her nine strings of necklaces.

Wait a second! thought acorn-Idun. *If that's Freya, then who's wearing her falcon feather cloak?*

Just then, the falcon flapped its wings. It was going to fly off again, with the apple-filled *eski* clasped in its claws!

"Not so fast, mister! Aren't you forgetting something?" Freya warned the falcon.

Mister? Huh? thought acorn-Idun.

"And where's Idun?" asked Skade and Sif.

Thor and several other boygods moved toward the falcon, surrounding it in case it tried to leave. "Oh, yeah, the cloak," said Loki's voice. *Loki?* Sure enough, when the wearer of the cloak shrugged it off, she saw for the first time that it was him. "Almost forgot. Here you go," he said, handing Freya's cloak back to her.

Idun could scarcely believe it. Her rescuer had been *Loki*? She felt like slugging him and hugging him at the same time. Only she was still a nut and didn't have arms!

"Where's Idun?" all three old women repeated.

"Here I am!" Idun called out to them from her perch on Ratatosk's open paw. But her friends, all of whose ears weren't so good anymore, didn't hear her.

Loki glanced down at the ground around him. "Oops. I must have accidentally dropped her. Has anyone seen an acorn about so big?" he asked, pinching his thumb and forefinger together and leaving an inch gap between them to indicate Idun's current small size.

"Over here! I've got her!" Ratatosk called out. He hopped up and down, as excited as if he'd just discovered he was holding the winning ticket to a lottery. "I thought she was one of my message acorns," he explained as he scurried over to Loki and handed acorn-Idun to him.

Loki grinned at acorn-Idun and then set her on the ground by his yellow shoes. "I bet you're surprised to see me!"

Before she could reply, Loki murmured some magic words and *poof* . . . Idun was instantly her girlgoddess self again.

14
Young Again

"**W**ELCOME BACK! WE WERE SO WORRIED about you," grandma versions of Freya, Skade, and Sif cried out to Idun.

"Yeah, ditto. Here's your *eski*," Loki said brightly, scooting her cart over to her. Idun just scowled at him. Any urge she'd felt to hug him had passed. So had the urge to slug him, but that did *not* mean that she was in a forgiving mood.

"Hey, everyone. Come and get 'em! Youth-restoring

golden apples!" Turning her back on Loki, she reached into her *eski* and began to hand around the apples of youth that remained in it to all who had aged in her absence, including Odin and Ms. Frigg. "I don't have enough for everyone, so just take a few bites and share these for now, okay? I'll pick more soon for dinner and for breakfast tomorrow. Promise!"

Though everyone showered her with gratitude, she barely had time to acknowledge their thanks. The most important thing now was to reverse the aging process that had occurred in them as quickly as possible.

Nevertheless, she paused in her task and did a double take when a bald old man with a long white beard wandered over. Catching her eye, he exclaimed, "As you probably knew, we were worried about you!"

Rhyme! Then this had to be . . . "Bragi?" she asked in astonishment.

It was just yesterday that she and her friends had come upon Loki and him on their way back from shopping and heard the boygods ask Heimdall how long it might take before they could grow beards. At the time the girls had laughed, trying to picture the two with hair on their chins. Who knew that only a day later, Bragi would be sporting not just the beginnings of a beard, but a long white one at that! Only now, him having a beard didn't seem so funny.

"That's my name, I'm one and the same!" Bragi replied. As if to prove it, he took a big bite of the apple. Instantly the added years melted away until he was restored to his former youthful self. Then he passed his apple to Thor, who also took some bites and instantly de-aged before passing the partly eaten apple on to yet another elderly student.

"I . . . um . . . I need to tell you something," Bragi said, following Idun as she moved on to distribute more apples from her *eski*. "While you were gone, I realized I might never get a chance to say it if you didn't come back, so . . ."

196

"Yeah?" she asked. Winding up her arm, she pitched an apple to two elderly girlgoddesses who were waving their hands to attract her attention.

Bragi reached into the *eski* and began helping her toss apples to more students. "I . . . uh . . . Do you remember how Loki teased me yesterday? About you being the apple of, um, you know, my eye?"

At the mention of Loki, Idun frowned. "Yes, but Loki says a lot of things that aren't true, so don't worry about—"

"Wait," Bragi interrupted her. "I . . . um . . ." Glancing around at the others near them, he lowered his voice so that only Idun would be able to hear him. "It's kind of true that I like you. I mean, *like*-like you." He rushed on. "You don't have to say anything. I just wanted you to know, that's all." Looking a little embarrassed now, he ran off, his energetic boy-self again thanks to her apples.

Stunned, Idun stood still and stared after him.

Slowly a smile bloomed on her face. "I like you, too," she admitted softly. She knew he wouldn't hear, and he didn't since he was pretty far away by now. Which was just as well. She needed to think about what he'd told her for a while. If a crush was destined to happen between them, it would unfold in its own good time. No rush.

"Hey! Over here," called Freya's brother, Frey. "Got any more apples?"

"Sure! Yes, sorry," said Idun, snapping back to attention. Happily, she continued distributing apples. Murmurs of relief and delight echoed around her as the prematurely aged were made young again. Gray hair turned blond, brown, red, or black. Wrinkles smoothed out into youthful skin. Whiskers disappeared. Hearing and sight improved.

Freya, Skade, and Sif had patiently waited for her to pass out her apples to all the others who needed them before accepting any themselves. So by the time Idun approached her friends, most everyone else had begun to head back to the academy.

She held up her one remaining apple. "Hope you don't mind sharing," she told them, already knowing they wouldn't. Freya had been carefully checking the feathers of her cloak, probably to make sure Loki hadn't damaged any, Idun guessed. Now she glanced up at Idun and smiled. So did Skade and Sif. One by one, each of the three girls took a big bite of the apple, and soon all three were restored to their former youth.

"Well, *that* was an interesting experience," Skade remarked wryly.

Laughing, the four girlgoddesses reunited joyfully in a huge group hug. When they finally released one another, Idun said hurriedly, "As much as I'd like to stay and talk, I'd better get to my grove to pick the rest of my apples. The V kitchen will need them for dinner tonight."

"We'll go with you," said Freya.

Before Idun could fold up her *eski*, Skade pointed to something down at the bottom of it, saying, "Wait, what's that?"

"Oh. They're tree bark sheets." Idun had almost forgotten about them. "With recipes I stole from Thiazi. I was hoping they'd give the Valkyries some fresh ideas for preparing my golden apples."

"Oh! Thank goodness!" blurted Skade with evident relief.

Freya and Sif quickly tried to shush her.

"Aha! I thought so. You guys are tired of my apples being served in the same ol' apple ways, aren't you?" Idun said. "You want different recipes."

"You're not upset?" asked Sif. "We didn't want to hurt your feelings by telling you. You're always trying to help everyone, and it seemed super mean to criticize."

Idun smiled. "Don't worry. Hopefully some of these new recipes will prove—" But as she reached into her *eski* to pick up the stack of bark sheets, her smile fell. They were charred and black. "Sparks from the fire at the wall must have leaped into my *eski* and burned them," she murmured. It was a wonder her apples hadn't caught fire too, but maybe their magic had protected them.

At any rate, the recipes were ruined. Totally unreadable. With a sigh, she tossed them to the ground where they would eventually turn to compost and become part of the cycle of life.

"So much for that idea, but I'll figure something out, I promise. I'm just relieved to be back, so I can tend to my trees and do my job." With a sigh, Idun picked up her *eski*, folded it to ice-cube size, and pocketed it.

"I'm curious. Why did you think it was a good idea to invite Loki to go with you to plant apple seeds?" Freya asked lightly as the four of them headed toward the grove.

Feeling embarrassed, Idun explained about her plan to help Loki improve his reputation by getting him to perform a good deed. "I should've known better," she finished. "He really is a bad apple."

"Rotten to the core!" Sif exclaimed.

"Don't feel too bad about what happened with Loki, though," Freya said. "He's fooled or tricked almost everyone here at the academy at one time or another."

"No kidding," said Sif, running a hand over her metallic hair.

"Yeah! That boy isn't just a rotten apple—he's a *worm* in a rotten apple!" said Skade.

They all laughed.

Freya smoothed the feathers on her cloak, which she still held over one arm. "I bet he would have kept my cloak just now if he could've gotten away with it."

Idun looked at the cloak wistfully. "Hard to blame him."

Her friends had come clean about their need for a wider variety of apple recipes. Now the urge to spill her feelings and come clean about everything *she'd* been holding back filled her. Words burst from her lips.

"When I saw that cloak in Glad Rags yesterday, I really, really, really wanted it," she told Freya.

"What?" Freya said in surprise. "But when I asked if you intended to buy it, you said—"

"That I didn't. Which wasn't true. I could tell how badly you wanted it," Idun said. "I didn't want to be selfish, so . . ."

"Speaking up for yourself isn't necessarily selfish," Freya said with a shake of her head.

"Yeah," Sif agreed. "Unless maybe you're Loki and you only consider yourself and never anyone else. But you aren't like that."

Freya held the cloak out to Idun. "If you still want it, it's yours. You saw it first. I'm happy to give it to you."

Idun reached out an eager hand, but then the look on Freya's face stopped her. She could tell how hard it was for her to make the offer. Freya loved this cloak. And it clearly loved her. Its feathers were ruffling in distress at the very idea of being parted from her. Looking from the cloak to Freya, Idun let her hand drop and slowly shook her head. "You keep it. You're the one it wants."

Freya smiled, looking relieved. "Thanks so much, Idun. You're the best. But if you ever want to borrow it, just say the word."

Idun glanced at the sky. The sun was starting to dip toward the horizon. "Yikes. It's almost time for dinner. The Valkyries will need those apples!" A sudden wish to try out the cloak at least once rose up in her. "Hey, Freya. The word."

"Huh?" Freya arched an eyebrow in confusion.

Idun grinned at her. "I'm saying 'the word.' Like you told me I should do to borrow your cloak. So can I borrow it now to get to the grove faster? After I've picked the rest of the apples, I'll catch up to you all at the Valhallateria in two shakes of a falcon's tail."

Freya's mouth curved into a huge smile. "Done," she said. Without hesitation, she handed over the cloak.

"Freya's friend," the cloak hummed happily as Idun

donned it. It seemed to understand that this was only a temporary loan, not a change in ownership, and so accepted what was going on.

Immediately Idun felt the cloak tighten around her. A tingly sensation ran through her as her feet became clawed and her head acquired a beak. How strangely light she felt as her feathery wings unfolded grandly from her sides! Her takeoff was a little wobbly and she dipped from one side to the other over and over.

"Try to center your core," Freya called up to her.

Center my core? The instruction confused Idun. But then she thought about how the flesh of an apple centered around *its* core, and the image helped her to regain her balance.

"Got it! Thanks," Idun called back. Only what came out of her mouth . . . uh, *beak* . . . was just a high-pitched shriek. *EeYEE!* With a *whoosh*, she was off to the grove while her friends continued on to the Valhallateria.

Wow! Even though she was way up high, Idun could

see things far below that she never could have seen if she hadn't been a falcon. She certainly hadn't been able to see this clearly as an acorn. Having falcon eyes was awesome! All kinds of details stood out. Especially anything moving. Like a little chipmunk she spied running across a boulder below her. Reveling in the ability to soar through the air under her own wing power, she circled the sky once, just for the joy of it, and then quickly flew to her grove.

After she landed, she took off Freya's cloak and carefully folded it over a tree branch, making sure not to injure its feathers. Hurriedly she unpocketed her *eski*, gave it a shake to enlarge it, and then set it on the ground. Working as fast as she could, she picked the remaining apples on her trees. She had just plucked the last apple when an eagle appeared and sailed down to land near her.

Thinking the eagle-giant had returned to kidnap her again, she raced for the falcon cloak, but then the eagle transformed into Loki. "You scared me half to death!" she yelled at him. "I thought you were Thiazi!"

"Oops, sorry," he said with that infuriatingly cocky grin of his. "My bad," he added, taking a seat on the edge of her *eski*.

"Yes, you *are* bad! A bad apple!" she scolded him. "You put your own welfare above mine and many others' at AA when you let that giant kidnap me. Talk about selfish! And dumb, too. Without my apples you would have grown old like everyone else!"

"True," Loki acknowledged. "I didn't think of that at the time I made the deal. It's hard to think clearly when you're in the clutches of a crazy eagle, being dragged over boulders and trees."

Idun had run out of sympathy for this boygod after his recent antics, so his words had no effect on her. "Yeah, tell me about it. I wound up in its clutches too, thanks to you!" She crossed her arms in front of her chest. "What hurts most is that I really believed you wanted to change. But it was all a lie. Just like that magic growing spell you claimed you were casting over the seeds we planted. That was really—"

"Whoa. Wait!" Loki interrupted. He rose from the edge of her *eski* to stand. "I admit I did some awful things," he said, looking her in the eye. "Still, I never meant to put your life—or anyone else's—in danger. I apologize for that. My magic spell wasn't a lie, though. And it worked. I've just been to Midgard to check on those seeds we planted. They've already sprouted and grown into saplings."

Frowning, Idun said, "And I should believe you because . . . ?"

A look of hurt flashed across Loki's face but was soon replaced by his customary smirk. He motioned to the feather cloak hanging from the branch. "If you don't believe me, you can go see for yourself."

"Ha!" she spat out. "And let you steal the apples in my *eski* while I'm gone?"

Clomp! Clomp! The sound of galloping horse hooves came toward them. Seconds later, Odin appeared in the grove upon the back of his horse, Sleipnir. The eight-legged gray foal had magically appeared in Asgard and was claimed by Odin not long after a boygiant named Mason, with the help of his superstrong horse, had repaired the wall around Asgard.

Odin, now his normal self again thanks to Idun's apples, reined in Sleipnir but didn't climb down from him. "I was gazing out over the nine worlds just now and saw you both fly here," he told Idun and Loki. "I came to congratulate you, Idun. Those seeds you planted are sprouting up all over Midgard. At the rate they're growing, they'll soon be bearing apples. I'm already hearing from grateful humans."

Idun looked at Loki in surprise. So he hadn't been lying about the saplings. No matter what other lies Loki had told, or the wrong he'd done to her and others at AA, Idun believed in giving credit where credit was due.

"Loki helped me plant them. It was his magic spell that caused the seeds to grow so fast," she told Odin.

"Is that so?" Odin gave Loki a look of pleased surprise. "Good for you," he said, leaning down and patting Loki on the shoulder. "Those new apple trees will not only add to the food supply for humans, but also to the health of the environment!"

Loki beamed at Odin's words. He seemed genuinely proud of this accomplishment and thrilled at Odin's approval.

"Good job rescuing Idun too, by the way," Odin said as he smoothed his horse's mane.

Loki flicked Idun a smile before replying. "Actually, Idun was already heading back to Asgard by the time I spotted her." He angled his gaze toward her. "How did you escape anyway?"

Quickly Idun explained how Thiazi had imprisoned her in the pantry of his mountaintop café before going fishing, and how she'd managed to pick the lock and escape. Odin laughed heartily at the "trick" she'd pulled on the giant, and Loki gave her an admiring look. "Clever," he said, nodding. Since Loki prided himself on his *own* cleverness, this was high praise, indeed.

Maybe Loki wasn't such a lost cause after all. She and others could continue to nudge him the direction of better behavior in the future. However, Idun realized that if this boygod ever truly changed, it would only be because he sincerely *wanted* to. In fact, this was probably the case for everyone—including her.

Then she thought of something else. "I'm not sure how Thiazi knew that Loki had transformed me into a nut to carry me back to Asgard," she said, craning her neck to look up at Odin. "But it doesn't seem like he would've chased Loki and me so hard if he hadn't known who we really were."

Odin laughed again. "He did. Giants like Thiazi can see through disguises."

"Oh!" Loki sounded surprised, like this was something

he hadn't known either, despite the fact that he was half-giant. "I was also carrying your *eski* in my other claw," he reminded Idun. "His eagle eye would've spotted that, too. He would've wanted to keep whatever magic apples he could."

Apparently growing bored with standing still, Sleipnir began to stamp his eight hooves and snort. "We'll be on our way soon," Odin soothed the horse. He eyed the apples in Idun's *eski*. "I imagine you want to get those over to the Valhallateria."

She nodded in reply and gave her *eski* a tap. Its sled runners dropped.

Meanwhile, Odin said to Loki, "Speaking of eagle eyes, I could use *yours*. Maybe you could help me out? I've just gotten a report that frost giants are gearing up to make trouble in Asgard. They haven't been much of a threat since Thor acquired Mjollnir, but I'm concerned now that they've just been regrouping. Could you do a little scouting and report back to me on whatever you discover?"

Loki's chest puffed out. Seeming pleased and honored to be asked, he replied, "You bet, O."

Idun's eyes rounded and she breathed in sharply. Had Loki really dared to nickname the great and powerful Odin . . . *O*? Right to his face?

Odin's eyebrows shot up. His one good eye stared hard at Loki. "What did you just call me?" he growled.

Loki grinned nervously. ". . . din! I meant Odin!" he said hurriedly. Then, looking worried that Odin might reconsider the wisdom of having asked him for help, the boy shape-shifted into an eagle and sailed off into the sky.

Odin winked at Idun. "He's less likely to cause mischief if we keep him busy with projects helping others, eh? And those giants really *are* a concern!" Without waiting for her to respond, he sent her a wave and zoomed off on his horse.

Idun stared after him and Sleipnir. Did Odin think she'd asked Loki to help her plant apple seeds in Midgard to keep him out of mischief? Even if that *had* been her plan, it wouldn't have worked. Because Loki had already had his *own* plan of turning her over to Thiazi!

She turned her head to look in the direction Loki had just disappeared. Was it really a good idea to send that boygod to spy on the frost giants? Odin knew how tricky Loki could be, right? He must know what he was doing, though. And she needed to get going!

Idun grabbed Freya's cloak from the tree where she'd hung it. As she carefully laid it across her *eski*, she noticed a thin, square piece of tree bark on the ground by her feet. One of Thiazi's burnt recipes. She must have missed that one when she'd tossed the rest. It had probably fallen to the ground when she'd taken her *eski* from her pocket to enlarge it earlier. She picked it up.

Hey! This one was scorched, but it was *not* ruined. The recipe's title was: The Make A Wish Apple Dish. Quickly she scanned the recipe, then reread it again with growing disbelief and excitement. The recipe was for a magical apple dish that would taste differently to whoever ate it. It would taste like the apple dish the person eating it most desired! To one person, it might taste like caramel apples, but to another, like apple fritters or applesauce or apple whatever.

This was perfect—exactly what she needed! *Do a good deed, and you'll get what you need.* That sweater in Glad Rags had been right after all. When she had tried to do a good deed in helping Loki, she just hadn't realized that what *she* needed wasn't the cloak. Instead, it was this recipe!

"Woo-hoo!" she shouted to the skies. She did a happy dance right then and there in her special grove under her nine wonderfully magical trees.

What an eventful weekend it had been, Idun thought as she pushed off for the V kitchen with her precious golden apples of youth. She'd been captured by a giant and escaped him. She'd gotten Loki to help her make new apple trees grow in Midgard. And she'd even experienced the beginnings of a crush . . . *maybe*. And now she'd wound up with this magical recipe! She could hardly wait to show the Valkyries and tell her friends.

Speaking of her friends, it usually seemed like they were the ones with big news and she was the quiet one. But for once, things were different. Her footsteps quickened. Settling into a rhythm, she glided her cart faster and faster. She couldn't wait to fill Freya, Skade, and Sif in on everything that had happened while the four of them had been apart.

Smiling as she slid along smoothly over the crisp, new-fallen snow, she imagined their happiness when they found out about this magical recipe too. She had a feeling everyone at Asgard Academy was going to love it. Her heart brimmed with joy. Her apples would be the apples of everyone's eyes. Hooray!

Authors' Note

To WRITE EACH BOOK IN THE THUNDER GIRLS series, we choose one or more Norse myths and then give them an updated middle-grade twist. After deciding on what elements we'll include from various retellings of the myths, we freely add interesting and funny details in order to create meaningful and entertaining stories we hope you'll enjoy.

We also write the Goddess Girls middle-grade series, which features Greek mythology. So why write another kind of mythology now too? Good question! Our enthusiasm for Norse mythology strengthened after Suzanne began frequent visits to her daughter and granddaughter, who live in Oslo, Norway. There, representations of the Norse gods and goddesses and their myths are found in many museums. Along the walls in the courtyard of the Oslo City Hall, there are painted wooden friezes (by painter and sculptor Dagfin Werenskiold) that illustrate motifs from various Norse myths. These friezes are the inspiration for the Valhallateria friezes that come alive at the end of meals in Thunder Girls!

We hope our series will motivate you to seek out actual retellings of Norse myths, which will also give you more understanding of and "inside information" about characters, myths, and details we've woven into Thunder Girls. Below are some of the sources we consult to create our stories.

- *D'Aulaires' Book of Norse Myths* by Ingri and Edgar Parin D'Aulaire (for young readers)
- *The Norse Myths* by Kevin Crossley-Holland
- *The Prose Edda* by Snorri Sturluson
- *The Poetic Edda* translated and edited by Jackson Crawford
- *Norse Mythology: A Guide to the Gods, Heroes, Rituals, and Beliefs* by John Lindow
- *Norse Mythology A to Z* by Kathleen N. Daly

For more about the art and friezes at Oslo City Hall, visit theoslobook.no/2016/09/03/oslo-city-hall.

Happy reading!

Joan and Suzanne

Acknowledgments

MANY THANKS TO OUR PUBLISHER, Aladdin/Simon & Schuster, and our editor, Alyson Heller, who gave an immediate and supportive yes to our idea to write a Norse mythology–based middle-grade series. Alyson also edits Goddess Girls, Heroes in Training, and Little Goddess Girls, our three ongoing Greek mythology–based series for children. We have worked with her for many years and feel very lucky to be doing all these series with her and the other fine folk at Aladdin. They help make our words shine, design fabulous art to make our books stand out, and make every effort to see that our books reach as many readers as possible.

We are also indebted to our literary agent, Liza Voges. She has championed us in all our joint series ventures and worked hard on our behalf and on behalf of our books. Thank you, Liza!

We are grateful to Danish artist Pernille Ørum for her striking covers for these books in our Thunder Girls series, and we look forward to more of her art.

Finally, we thank our husbands, George Hallowell and Mark Williams, for offering advice when asked, troubleshooting computer problems, and just making our lives richer and easier. During hectic times in our writing schedules they're always good sports, taking up the slack of daily chores without complaint.

Glossary

NOTE: **PARENTHESES INCLUDE INFORMATION** specific to the Thunder Girls series.

Aesir: Norse goddesses and gods who live in Asgard

Alfheim: World on the first (top) ring where light-elves live

Angerboda: Loki's giantess wife whose name means "distress-bringer" (angry Asgard Academy student and girlgiant)

Asgard: World on the first (top) ring where Aesir goddesses and gods live

Bifrost Bridge: Red, blue, and green rainbow bridge built by the Aesir from fire, air, and water

Bragi: God of poetry (student at Asgard Academy and boygod)

Breidablik Hall: Hall of the Norse god Balder (boys' dorm at Asgard Academy)

Brising: Freya's necklace, shortened from *Brísingamen* (Freya's magic jewel)

Darkalfheim: World on the second (middle) ring where dwarfs live

Draupnir: Magical golden arm-ring that the dwarfs make as a gift for Odin

Dwarfs: Short blacksmiths in Darkalfheim (some young dwarfs attend Asgard Academy)

Eski: Wooden box made of ash wood in which Idun keeps her apples of youth

Fire giants: Terrifying giants who live in Muspelheim

Frey: Vanir god of agriculture and fertility whose name is sometimes spelled Freyr, brother of Freya (Freya's twin brother and Asgard Academy student and boygod)

Freya: Vanir goddess of love and fertility (Vanir girlgoddess of love and beauty who is an Asgard Academy student)

Frigg: Goddess of marriage, who is Odin's wife (coprincipal of Asgard Academy with Odin)

Frost giants: Descendants of Ymir from Jotunheim

Gladsheim Hall: Sanctuary where twelve Norse gods hold meetings (Asgard Academy's assembly hall)

Gullveig: Vanir sorceress whose gold-hunting in Asgard causes the Aesir-Vanir war (Freya and Frey's nanny and library assistant at the Heartwood Library)

Gungnir: Magical spear that the dwarfs made as a gift for Odin

Hangerock: Sleeveless apronlike dress, with shoulder straps that are fastened in front by clasps, that is worn over a long-sleeved linen shift

Heidrun: Goat that produces mead for the fallen warriors in Valhalla (the ceramic goat fountain in the Valhallateria)

Heimdall: Watchman of the gods (security guard at Asgard Academy)

Helheim: World on the third (bottom) ring inhabited by the evil dead and ruled by a female monster named Hel

Hlidskjalf: Odin's throne

Honir: Long-legged Aesir god known for his indecisiveness

Hugin: One of Odin's two ravens whose name means "thought"

Idun: Aesir goddess who is the keeper of the golden apples of youth (Asgard Academy student and girl-goddess)

Jotunheim: World on the second (middle) ring where frost giants live

Kenning: Nickname made up of two descriptive words connected by a hyphen

Kvasir: Vanir god sent to Asgard at the end of the Aesir-Vanir war who offered helpful information (Asgard Academy student and boygod from Vanaheim)

Light-elves: Happy Asgard Academy students from Alfheim

Loki: Troublemaking, shape-shifting god of fire (Asgard Academy student and boygod)

Midgard: World on the second (middle) ring where humans live

Mimir: Wise Aesir god who was beheaded and revived by Odin ("head" librarian at Asgard Academy)

Mjollnir: Mighty hammer made for Thor

Munin: One of Odin's two ravens whose name means "memory"

Muspelheim: World on the third (bottom) ring where fire giants live

Nidhogg: Dragon that lives in Niflheim and gnaws at the root of the World Tree

Niflheim: World on the third (bottom) ring where the good dead are sent

Njord: Vanir god of the sea sent to Asgard after the Aesir-Vanir war (Asgard Academy student and boygod from Vanaheim)

Norse: Related to the ancient people of Scandinavia, a region in Northern Europe that includes Denmark, Norway, and Sweden and sometimes Finland, Iceland, and the Faroe Islands

Odin: Powerful Norse god of war, wisdom, and poetry who watches over all nine worlds (coprincipal of Asgard Academy with his wife, Ms. Frigg)

Ragnarok: Prophesied doomsday when goddesses and gods will fight a fiery battle against evil that could destroy all nine Norse worlds

Ratatosk: Squirrel that runs up and down Yggdrasil spreading gossip and insults

Sif: Golden-haired goddess of the harvest (Asgard Academy student and girlgoddess)

Skade: Goddess of skiing, sometimes spelled Skadi (Asgard Academy student and half-giant girl)

Skidbladnir: Magical ship made as a gift for Frey

Sleipnir: Odin's eight-legged horse

Spydkast: A competition that involves throwing a spear as far as possible after running

Thiazi: Giant who forces Loki to bring him Idun and her apples

Thor: Superstrong Norse god of thunder and storms (Asgard Academy student and boygod)

Trolls: Subgroup of giants who live in Ironwood Forest near Midgard (barefoot troublemakers at Bifrost Bridge)

Valhalla: Huge room in Asgard where dead warriors feast and fight (Valhallateria is Asgard Academy's cafeteria)

Valkyries: Warrior maidens in winged helmets who choose which warriors will die in battle and then bring them to Valhalla (cafeteria ladies and workers in Asgard Academy's Valhallateria)

Vanaheim: World on the first (top) ring where Vanir goddesses and gods live

Vanir: Norse goddesses and gods who live in Vanaheim

Vingolf Hall: Goddesses' meeting hall at Asgard (girls' dorm at Asgard Academy)

Yggdrasil: Enormous ash tree that links all nine ancient Norse worlds, also called the World Tree (location of Asgard Academy)

Ymir: Very first frost giant whose body parts were used to create the Norse cosmos, including mountains, the sea, and the heavens